A SCAR IN THE SKY

M. A. COLE

A SCAR IN THE SKY

ISBN: 978-0-578-46718-4

Dedication

To my family,

I can't thank you all enough for teaching me how to love so that I could pass your blessed and wholehearted lessons on myself. What greater gift could anyone receive? I realize we are all getting a little older now and my prayer for every one of us is to find and keep peace in our hearts, no matter what we're going through, where we are or what we're doing. I'm praying that this life is just the beginning of so many more beautiful things to come. I feel very much the same way as our beautiful Nanny used to say, "I may only have a dollar in my pocket but if I have my family, that's enough for me."

I love you all!

Before It's Too Late

In such a precocious age
so many choose to carelessly
take one side over another.

When was it forgotten that
the rich, the poor, the black,
white, brown and yellow
all came from a mother?

Are we truly that different
or at the core, wouldn't it be
we all want the same?

Depending on who is listened to
is who actually guides much,
if not all of the blame.

When do we become that much intended one
or do we delay until it's too late?

Seems such a useless waste
of life, love and time,
this thing we so easily call hate

M. A. Cole

Table of Contents

The Key to Life

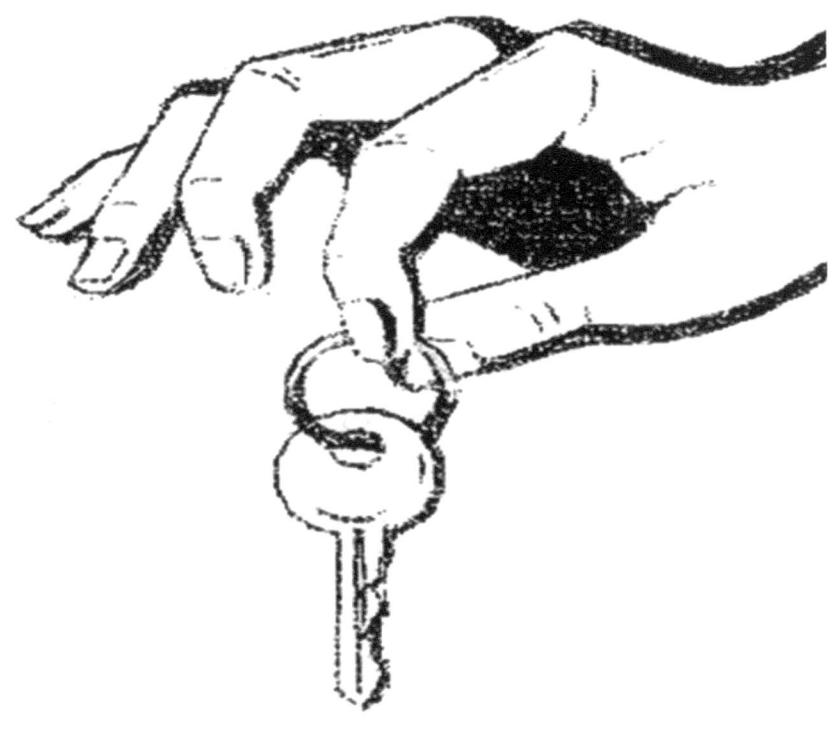

John Lennon once told a story about when he was a young boy his mother taught him that happiness was the key to life. Later, after he started school, he was given an assignment where he was asked to answer the question, "What do you want to be when you grow up?" Remembering his mother's life lesson, John, in absolute certainty answered the question with one simple word, "Happy." His teacher and classmates more or less made fun of his seemingly over-simplistic answer. They told him that he must not have fully understood the assignment. He then, in his purest conviction assured them all that they were actually the ones who didn't understand life's real assignment or its true purpose.

My younger brother Samuel—Sammy, as we called him—definitely understood what that famous Beatle was saying, even if at times it didn't seem like he understood much else. Sammy was the middle of us three brothers. There was me, Israel; I am the oldest. Sammy, our middle brother and Jacob, our youngest brother. Unlike Jacob or I, Sammy was born with Down Syndrome. In Sammy's first five years of life and several times afterwards, he had many surgeries to attempt to fix everything from his heart to a multitude of other intestinal problems but regardless of any of the health issues that he may have faced along the way, he was definitely the glue that held our family together.

There's a beauty to Down Syndrome that not many people speak about or even know. There's an innocence that seems to block most, if not all of the externally bad elements that most so-called normal people experience out of the lives of those who were born in such a way. In Sammy's case, to confirm these thoughts, he always had this particular look in his eye. This look signaled to the world that he was greater than any problem life threw at him. It was a look that let everyone know that he had something very special about him and that beautiful something didn't have anything to do with an extra chromosome. His surgeries and the majority of his health problems eventually slowed down and from that point he was more or less free to be that gleaming light to everyone who ever met him.

Our parents never let us or really anyone ever treat him any differently than anyone else. At times, we all may have had to be a little more patient but for the most part, Sammy was just as much of an adventurous little boy as any other child was. All of us brothers were a little more than a year apart in age and eventually, when we started going to school, Sammy had his classes and we had ours but either Jacob or myself would always get him for lunch and after school every day. We did this, not only to make sure he was okay but also to make sure he wasn't getting into any more trouble than we were.

Sammy was never picked on or treated poorly by anyone, not around the neighborhood or in school. One reason was because Jacob or I were never too far away but more importantly, because everyone loved him. Whether he was in their class or not, all of the students and teachers always seemed to brighten up when he was around, just like we did as his family. Sammy had such a genuine and caring personality and he always warmly greeted everyone he met with the phrase, "Good day." I don't know where he got that from. I'm guessing he probably heard it from a movie somewhere along the way but for whatever reason, it stuck. What was even funnier was, many of those people he welcomed often copied his refreshing salutation no matter where we were.

I felt like we were in England or somewhere with all of the formal-sounding "good days" that went around wherever we went. That special something that Sammy had most definitely allowed him to enjoy everything and everyone, regardless of where he was or what he was doing. His joy was so extremely contagious that it seemed to permeate through whomever he was around as well. Sammy's absolute favorite thing to do was going fishing.

This was something that he and I definitely had very much in common.

What made it easier is that we lived near the James River in Richmond, Virginia and often partook in our favorite pastime together at that wonderful place. The second great commonality Sammy and I had was participating in any kind of art project that we could. He loved painting and working with clay and things like that, and just like fishing, so did I. Even as young boys, the two of us just jelled. We'd either sit on the bank of that river for hours and hours fishing or we'd enthrall ourselves in whatever art project we were working on for what seemed like weeks at a time. No matter what we did, we always seemed to include some of the most profound conversations of my life.

When fishing at the river, we would talk while looking at the clouds, pretending like they were animals or people or parts of people, but we'd always get around to the fishing part of our fishing trip and it was usually pretty fruitful as well. Sometimes we just took our cane poles to catch as many brim as we could but other times we took much bigger rods to attempt to get at some of those much sought-after bass or catfish out of that wonderfully historic river. Sammy would often fiddle with the bait and sometimes even name the little grub worms that we used before he—or should I say, I—put them on his hook.

As a proud brother, I can say he always caught just as many fish as I ever did, if not more, even though he usually only had his line in the water about half the time that I did. Sammy had an ease with life that I've never seen with anyone else. I always admired his peaceful soul and at times I was probably even a little jealous of his relaxed disposition about almost everything. My youngest brother, Jacob and I definitely didn't share Sammy's peaceful experience. We often acted our grievances and frustrations out on each other. As much as Sammy got along with everyone, my youngest brother and I did not in regards to each other. I don't know what it was. I guess we were just born to be polar opposites, but regardless of the reasons, we seemed to fight all the time and it was almost from the first day that Jacob learned how to talk.

The first and most consistent word Jacob ever spoke was "no," and for some reason, he always looked and pointed directly at me when he said it. I never knew what I did to make him dislike me so much from such an early age but for whatever reason, he just didn't want anything to do with me and so often let me know it, too. At first, my parents thought our little youthful squabbles were funny, but over time, they became worse and even more serious.

It's not that we never got along. We had our moments of toleration, but for the most part, any full-fledged sibling peace was quite a rarity.

Even though Jacob never liked fishing or art or really anything else that I did, he would participate in another activity that Sammy really enjoyed. All of us boys would look up at the sky and pretend the clouds were animals or people or really anything that Sammy or the rest of us wanted them to be. Other than those times, Jacob spent a lot of time with Sammy on his own, too. It was rarely when I was around but he also had his own very special relationship with our middle brother in his own way. Jacob was just as protective and loving as anyone was with Sammy, it's just that for some unknown reason, none of his feelings ever transferred to me. I must have done something very wrong to that kid in a past life or somewhere because, for the life of me, I couldn't figure out what his lifelong issue with me was.

To make matters worse, we all shared a bedroom and my bed was located right in the middle of where both of my brothers slept. I can remember rolling over in the middle of the night and looking over at Sammy. He always had this look of contentment and happiness on his face which always warmed my heart even at a young age. Then I'd roll back over in the other direction towards Jacob.

Even though I knew early on he probably didn't know what it meant, he still for some reason slept with his middle finger stretched in the air and it always seemed to be pointing directly at me.

Being the oldest brother, I was often left in charge, if you could call it that. Because Sammy had a lot of medical bills, my parents really didn't have any other choice but to work a lot. Both my mother and father had two jobs and many times, from an early age, I was left to watch over my two younger siblings simply because they couldn't afford to get anyone else to do the job. I can't say it was always fun but I will say, whether it was Sammy, Jacob or even myself, something unexpected always seemed to happen and I was always responsible for it.

Butt Whippings

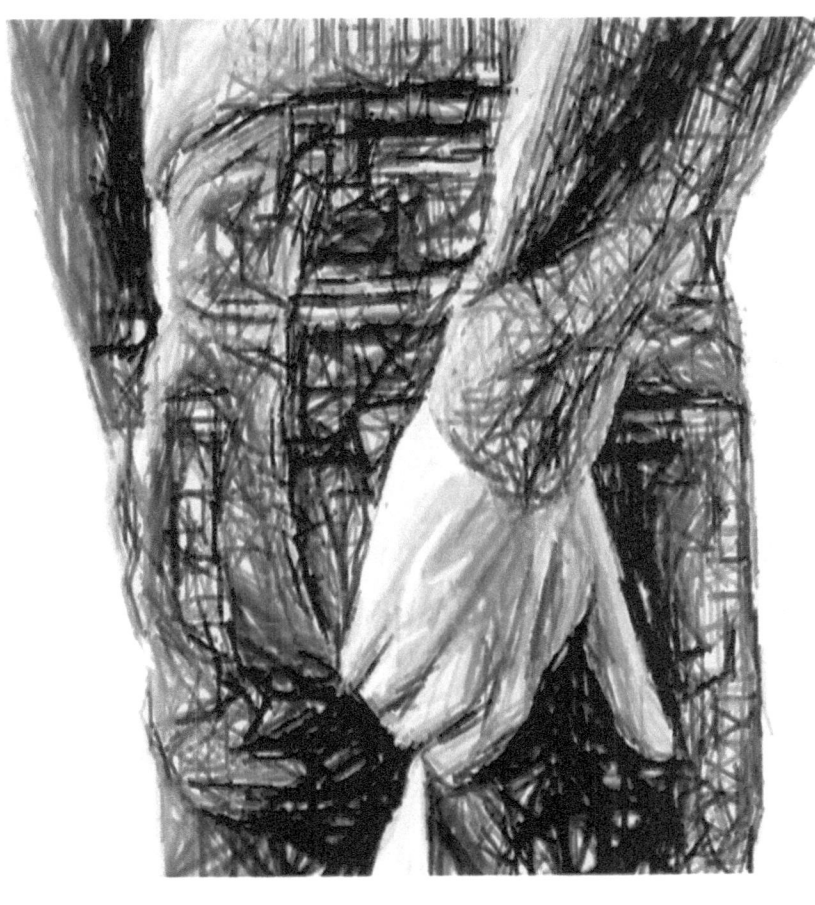

The one rule that my mother did have about togetherness was, we all had to sit down for dinner together as a family. My mom was off from her second job by dinner time and my dad would almost always come home to eat and then go back to work after the meal. This was a chance for our parents to catch up on whatever their children were doing and, of course, a time to interject some parental guidance before we did something stupid—or should I say, something else stupid—or disappointing to them once again. My mother never allowed the television on or for us to have any distractions during our forced family times. That was okay, though, because it seemed her boys always provided them with plenty to talk about anyway.

Being the oldest, I always tried to help out as much as I could, not only because my mother told me to, but also because Sammy was a handful at times. In reality, I knew we all were a little more than that most of the time. Our parents spent as much time as they could with us, but understandably, as much time as they could with Sammy. They really did do the best they could and we all knew they did, too. I really felt for my father. He worked what seemed like all the time. Looking back, I can't ever remember a time that we went without anything but he just had to work so much to make it that way.

He was a proud man who was bound and determined to work his way out of his family's financial hardships, even if it cost him so much precious time with us. My dad was a meat cutter by trade. He worked in the most winter-like surroundings almost all the time. He'd come home with his hands so swollen from the constant cold and often so tired that he could barely make it through our family meals and back to work again. The only part of any day that I can ever remember him taking off from work was on Sunday evenings. Most of that time, he'd try to catch up on his greatly deprived and much needed sleep. Being that my father was either gone or asleep most of the time, my mother was our definite and declared disciplinarian.

It's not that we were bad, but they had two boys who had a great amount of distain for one another and quite simply, things were bound to happen, as they often did. Many times, Jacob would wait until he saw our mother's old, green beat-up Monte Carlo pull in the driveway, then he would go towards the coat closet by the front door. When he heard our mother's, key enter the door knob, he'd start hitting himself almost to the point of drawing blood and then hide in the closet until she came in the door. That little jerk would then jump out of the closet, blaming me for hitting him and putting him in the closet in the first place.

I think Sammy thought it was a game that Jacob always played on me but it wasn't. We had an old-school mother; eye for an eye, butt whipping for hitting a brother kind of mother and that's often what I got, a butt whipping. I must have gotten a thousand whippings because of Jacob's theatrics, all while both of my brothers just sat there laughing at me and my pain. I always retaliated to Jacob's trickery whether it was a wise decision to do so or not. Sometimes it was immediate, sometimes I'd take a week or longer to plan it out but I always got him back in some way. One of my favorite acts of retaliation was during one of the coldest winter days of the year.

My mother had left her usual chore list for all of her sons to complete before she got home. Sammy's list usually only included putting the dishes away; the same one's that we dared not leave in the sink in the first place but he was included nonetheless. My chore list always seemed to be the longest. I guess because I was the oldest, but Jacob's chores always included taking out the trash. On this particular day, I decided to reciprocate some revenge on my least favorite fan. Back then, my father always made us take a shovel and push the trash down so we would be able to pack in as much as we could. He did this so the trash could be picked up every two weeks instead of every week like most people.

Understandably, if it saved him a little money, that's the route he was going to take. That day, I knew Jacob was going to have to lean all the way over to push all of that nasty trash way down to the bottom of the big can that we had at the time. It was no more than ten degrees outside and the stage was set because I knew my mother would be home soon and that meant Jacob had to be on his way outside within a very short period of time. I wrapped Sammy in his warmest jacket and then opened the upstairs window in our parents' bedroom so we could climb out on the roof. That past Christmas, I received a pretty strong BB gun and decided I was going to use that air rifle to inflict some pain on my brother who so often caused mine.

I made up my mind that day to hunt me some retaliatory Jacob butt. As Jacob leaned way over in the trash can, following my father's wishes to compact it down as much as he could, I fired off six rounds that I know for a fact reached their intended meaty target. I could tell that every pellet peppered each butt cheek with a fierce and unexpected equal bite. He was screaming and jumping around holding his backside as if he was stung by a million bees. Sammy was laughing so hard I thought he was going to fall off of the roof and, in truth, so was I.

Jacob didn't see where the sneak attack came from but he definitely knew without a shadow of a doubt that it was from me. As comical as that was, I fully accepted the logic that the retaliation I delivered on that cold day would bring a spanking that was very much worth getting. Looking back, we had so many of those back and forth interactions that events like that really were commonplace in our household. When we were bad enough, my father would get called in for back-up but our memories of whatever punishment we got never lasted too long because we were always back at it again almost each and every day. One time my retaliation almost scared me as much as it did Jacob.

It was raining outside, so the three of us were stuck in the house. Jacob and I were fighting, as usual, over some video game or something stupid. Sammy was once again laughing at his ignorant brothers while watching the tension grow. Jacob, as he always did, waited until the last minute to take out the trash. Since I long since had my BB gun taken away, I felt I had to do something at least similar to that scale and I had to do it then because he had been one-upping me for quite a while. As he went to the back yard to take out the trash before our mother came home, I went to the front yard to try and quickly figure out something to do to him.

I'd been fishing earlier in the week with some of my friends and they left an oar in our front yard. I then had the final draft of my new plan concocted. I thought it would be a good idea for some reason to throw that oar over the house to hopefully scare Jacob. Even I didn't think that oar that flew over the house so easily would hit him directly on his forehead with such a great and damaging smack, the outcome of my hasty idea resulted in Jacob being completely knocked the hell out. He laid motionless in the back yard with his arms and legs spread out as far as they could stretch. I wanted to get back at him for all of his constant crap but never to actually hurt him but so much.

Once again, Sammy was cracking up, but I wasn't. I was scared that Jacob was hurt pretty badly. Even though he didn't like me, I really didn't dislike him and I definitely didn't want to seriously injure him—especially right before my mother got home. For some reason, I didn't think I had any chance in hell of actually hitting him with that oar that I just flung over the house so easily but when I heard that loud smack, I knew that oar did a little more than what I had intended it to. Jacob eventually woke up after what seemed like an hour and when he did, he just shook his head.

As he sat up, he didn't say a word but he did look at me with these squinty eyes which seemed to tell say, "You SOB, it's on now." That was the first time that he didn't tell on me but he didn't have to. When my mother got home, it wasn't Jacob waiting at the door, it was Sammy. His first words to our mother were, "Israel knocked the hell out of Jacob with an oar." He was a little more explanatory than that but my mother knew we were at it once again. This time, though, instead of getting after me as she usually did, she was more worried about Sammy saying "hell" and spent the majority of her efforts correcting him. I felt like I kind of got away with that one but, in truth, I think that scared Jacob and I both to the point that we took a little break from our shenanigans for a while.

From that point on, more so than messing with each other, as we always seemed to do, Jacob turned his efforts to trying to outdo me in everything instead. If I scored a touchdown in a football game, he would score two. If I— which I often did—got a C on a paper or a test, he would get an A. One time, when I broke my finger, he seemed to make sure he broke his wrist a few weeks later. There was no limit to how badly Jacob wanted to beat me at everything. It was simply unexplainable to me but, for some reason, that's just the way our relationship was.

Lying down on our backs, looking up at the sky with Sammy was virtually the only time we all had any sort of common ground when it came to each other. Sammy liked looking at the sky and the clouds so much that we tried to put all of our differences aside long enough to make the one good brother we had as content as possible during those times. I know we shouldn't have taken Sammy in that direction but, because of our teenage minds and our influence on him, our favorite sightings in the clouds were those that we told him—and he'd later commonly say— were "boobies" in the sky. When he spotted what he knew to be a pair, he'd yell out, "Look, those are big ones!" Or, "Man, oh man, I see them shaking now!"

Those were times when it was our turn to laugh at Sammy and with him, too. When Jacob and I fought, Sammy never took sides. He was just there rooting both of us on. He didn't really care who won or not, he was just amused by watching his two idiot brothers half kill each other. Sammy was so different from us. He just didn't seem to experience the anger, frustration or even jealously like we obviously did.

He had such a peaceful nature that, even his embattled brothers would take a break every now and then for a while from fighting to make sure we weren't doing anything that may upset him too much. He didn't realize he was any different from anyone else but he definitely was, he was better; especially better than both of his ignorant brothers.

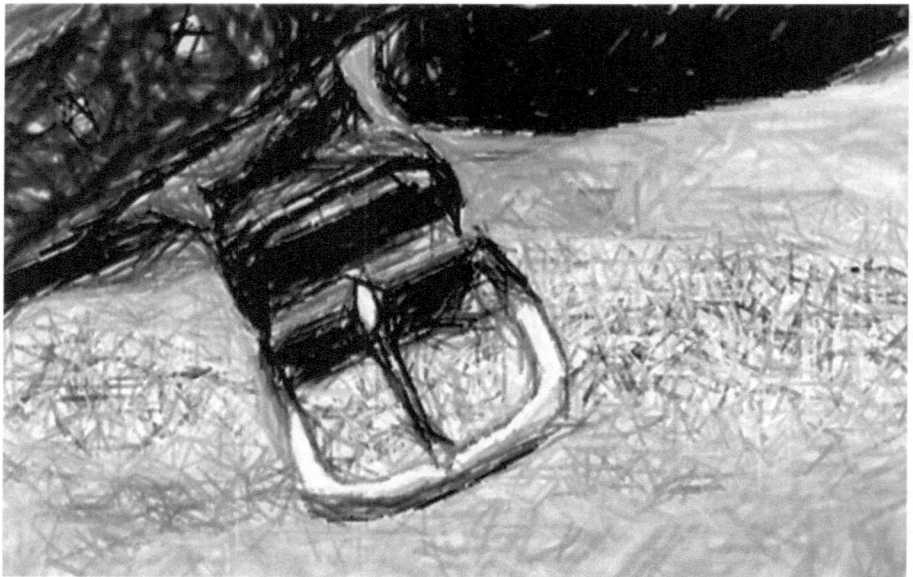

Bad Boys, Bad Boys

After a long hiatus of experiencing as much of a truce as Jacob and I could have, Jacob, out of nowhere, thought it would be funny to throw a fire cracker down at my feet. This wasn't any sort of ordinary firecracker either, it was an M-80. He could have blown my foot off, but unlike the oar incident where I didn't try to hurt him, I was mad enough to put his lights out. I never hit Jacob with my fists until that day and when I did, I beat him pretty good. Little to my knowing and since our backyards butted up to an elderly couple's house who seemed to creepily always be outside watching everything that ever happened, I did it right in front of them, too.

The old man stumbled over to the edge of his yard as fast as he could. When he finally got there, he started yelling at me to stop. I stopped when he asked me to, even though I thought Jacob deserved a little more. I was mad at Jacob but I was more scared about what that old man was going to tell my mother when she got home. As I followed the old man's wishes to stop beating my brother, Jacob was looking for a weapon that he quickly found and started to use. He got that stupid shovel that he so often used to push the trash down with and began beating me with it in his own attempts of retaliation.

He hit me with that stupid shovel to the point that I couldn't just stand there and get beaten to death by a garden tool, so I started fighting back again. It was so bad that the older lady called the police. The men in blue and my mother arrived at our house at almost the exact same time. We weren't grown men at this time but we weren't far off. We were both in high school and fairly stout and could have very well hurt each other pretty substantially. I still didn't think whatever we could have done to each other was going to be anything compared to what my mother was going to do to us now that her and the police were in our driveway. When my mother pulled up, seeing the look of absolute fear in her eyes was probably the worst punishment that we could ever receive.

She was definitely not a crier by any means; I've probably only seen her cry one time in my life before then and that was at my grandfather's funeral but this time, she was bawling from fear for her boys. She got out of the car and went rushing around looking for Sammy first. When she realized he was okay, she then came over to Jacob and me. She spun each one of us around one by one to make sure we didn't have any bones or anything like that sticking out of our bodies. Once she realized we were somewhat okay, her facial expression completely changed to one of absolute disappointment.

A bad beating from her would have been better than that look of shame that she gave us. To make matters worse, my father quickly screeched into the driveway a few minutes later. I'm sure my mother called him and he probably wanted to see for himself what his almost grown sons had done this time. My parents spoke with the policemen by themselves for a few minutes and then they left in their cruisers, most likely to their next domestic disturbance of the day. My parents may have kept us out of the pokey that day but what we got was much worse. My mother had always been so quick to respond in some kind of physically whipping sort of way, but not this time.

We'd long since been what most consider too big to get a whipping and in truth, it stopped hurting a long time ago, but that's what she was taught, so that's what she gave. This time, however, there was none of that. She didn't want to talk to or even look at Jacob or me. She was so upset that she didn't bother with the normal questions of who started it or what happened. She and my father just took Sammy in the house and slammed the door behind them, leaving Jacob and I very much locked outside. This was as serious as anything we'd ever done. We hurt her so badly once again like we'd probably been doing for such a long time, but this time she'd had enough.

As Jacob and I sat outside on the porch waiting to see if our mother would ever let us back in the house again, Sammy was at the window waving at us. He knew that we were in trouble but our little buddy seemingly missed us not being inside with him. While outside, Jacob and I both agreed that we didn't have to like each other but we couldn't hurt our parents like we did that day anymore either. When our mother finally let us back in the house, we had also decided that I would move out of our bedroom and I made a place for myself in the attic. That was probably something I should have done a long time ago but maybe that way we wouldn't be tempted to constantly mess with one another all of the time. Seeing my mother so disappointed broke my heart and I know even though Jacob probably blamed me for everything, it probably did his as well.

She Gave Me Poo

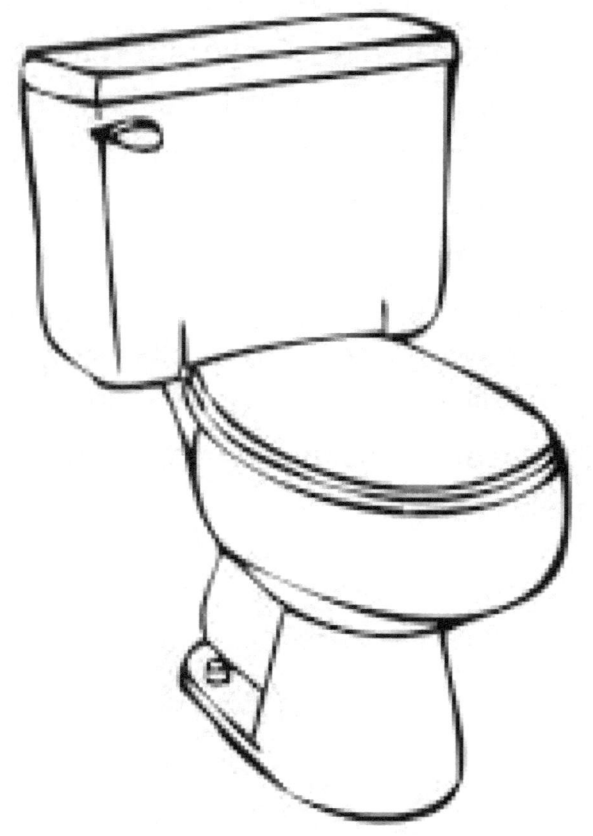

A t this point, I was going to be graduating in another six months and hopefully off to college soon after, so all of those years of that constant battling and sibling rivalry would be over soon anyway. Christmas wasn't too far off and now that my mother's disappointment seemed to subside, she was fully engaged in the holiday season as she was every year. She loved Christmastime. Now, we never per se wanted for anything, but we didn't have all of the nicer new things that many of our more well-to-do friends had either. Christmas was the one time that my mother would treat us all like kings. Sometimes I thought that was the real reason that her and my father worked all of the time like they did.

I honestly felt they worked so hard throughout the year so they could give us such wonderful things on that blessed day. None of us ever really cared about what we got, we were just very happy to get to spend some substantial time together as a whole family during the holiday season. Sammy always woke up first on Christmas morning and his job was to wake everyone else up. This was a job that he mastered throughout the year so it was a simple assignment for him to do on Christmas day as well.

Just watching Sammy on such an exciting day with the church songs, mouth-watering food and him opening his gifts would have been enough for any of us, but not for my mother. She always went over the top. She had a certain way of doing things on Christmas Day and everyone knew not to mess with her rhythm of that very special family day. She'd make everyone unwrap their presents one at a time so the others watching could partake in the excitement of the gift and the happiness of the recipient. I think in reality she was just trying to extend the day that was so precious to her. Sammy always went first on the smaller gifts, and like most kids, along with the stuff he really liked, he'd also get some necessities like underwear and socks. When Sammy got to those even, he couldn't pretend to be but so excited.

He'd open those presents in full excitement and if those certain things were inside, he'd say, "Oops, undies or sockies," then he'd quickly say, "Next up." He wasn't fooling anyone. He wanted everyone else to hurry up so he could open something else that he might like a little bit better than socks or underwear. As we opened our gifts, Sammy always kept us running as efficiently as possible. If he thought we were taking a little too much time with our own presents he would once again yell out, the ever familiar, "next up." Out of respect and love for our most seasonally excited brother, we'd hurry along.

My mother always felt she needed to be completely fair to all of her sons for some reason. She had to spend the exact same amount on each one of us as if we would feel less loved if there would have been an extra ten-dollars spent in one direction over the other, so on many years Christmas day was quite long. That simply wasn't what we felt at all but that's what she insisted on doing, so as most things that she wanted for us, we just said, "Yes ma'am" and followed her plans. The other thing that our mother did every Christmas day was she would pretend like all of the presents were opened and then she'd start cleaning up.

When she was almost finished cleaning, she'd say, "Boys, I believe I forgot something." This happened every year so we always knew it was coming. Sammy knew this too because his "next ups" became a little louder and more frequent when he felt the expected time was coming near. My mother would always hide our last gifts--"the big gift," as she called them—somewhere in the house or garage. We all knew that both of our parents worked their fingers to the bone for us and it really didn't matter what we got for Christmas but all of the gifts were appreciated, especially the big ones.

Christmas was the one day that Jacob and I didn't think about fighting, but more importantly, it was a day where we all truly seemed to fully and thoroughly enjoy each other's company. That year, Jacob got a used car. It may have only been a thousand-dollar Toyota but it was every bit as nice as what my mother or father or even I was driving at the time. They bought me a Jon boat that year. They knew I loved fishing, as did Sammy, so I couldn't have asked for a more thoughtful and useful gift. Unlike what she called the smaller gifts, my mother always made Sammy wait until last to open his big gift. I think that's the way she always wanted to remember our Christmases each year, so that's what happened.

When it was Sammy's turn, he discovered his present wasn't large in size like Jacob's or mine was, nor was it hidden in the garage like ours was either. My mother told Sammy to go check in the bathroom for his last and final gift of the year. We all laughed as Sammy looked back at our mother in shock because he had never had to look for a present in the bathroom before. He wanted to make sure she told him the correct directions so he said, "Are you sure it's in the bathroom, mom?" My mother giggled and then confirmed that she was very sure where she put it. Sammy ran down the hall to the bathroom and came out about a second later.

He yelled out, "You got me poo!" No one realized that he was the last one in there before that and he had unknowingly left his own self a present, but it wasn't the one that my mother was talking about. As Sammy flushed the toilet even my father was cracking up at his colorful and very animated middle child. My mother made her directions a bit more clear as she told Sammy to look in the tank of the toilet. Sammy used to play in the toilet bowl tank for some reason so he then knew very well where to find his big gift of the year. This sounds like a crazy place to hide something but for my mother, believe it or not, places like that were more of the norm than anywhere else.

When Sammy came back in the living room where everyone else was, he was holding a plastic bag with some kind of tickets inside. When he opened the bag, he noticed a picture of Mickey Mouse plastered across them and yelled out, "We're going to Disney World!" He was extremely excited because my mom decided to spend a little time with just him. The happiest kid in the world and his mother were going to the happiest place in the world. My mother always surprised all of us like that, even if at times we had to look in the toilet to find the gift.

I don't care what age you are, everyone loves Disney World and his favorite part of it was Animal Kingdom. Ever since Sammy was small, he loved animals of all kinds. Even with that BB gun he'd never let me shoot anything but targets and Jacob's butt that day. He even made me throw all of the fish that we ever caught back. In his words, we had to throw them back so they could "live on." I don't think he ever thought about the worms and what happened to them but I never had the heart to tell him either. While they were away, Jacob and I for the most part stayed away from each other.

We still didn't want to take a chance of hurting our mother again even when she was away and also because my dad was a little more in charge than usual so we dared not do too much. Our parents did so much for us for Christmas that we were going to at least try to act grown while she was gone. Jacob seemed to be mad at me for one reason or another his whole life and I simply never understood why. I was not without fault because I'd often instigate his displeasure with me to the point where we'd actually start fighting but, in my opinion, if his attitude would have been a bit different towards me, who knows how well we could have gotten along.

I think deep down we did care about each other but we rarely, if ever, showed it. Our relationship bothered me, it really did, but I never knew how to fix it and Jacob always pushed me past the point of wanting to try, so I didn't. We missed our mom the week she was gone but all of us secretly missed Sammy even more. The house just wasn't the same without either one of them but especially with Sammy being gone. When they finally returned, Sammy quickly and excitedly filled us in on all of their magical adventures, especially those that were related to animals in any way. He told us about the safari that they went on and all of the exotic birds and fish that they saw.

My mother knew at least one of her boys was totally grateful and extremely happy. Sammy definitely enjoyed himself but we were definitely just as grateful they were back home. It would soon be spring and then I would get a chance to take my Christmas present out as well. Fishing season was right around the corner and that was another thing that Sammy was going to be almost as excited about. This time, instead of fishing from the bank, we got to go out in my new Jon boat. I knew life jackets would be a must, they even were when we fished from the bank, but he didn't mind it. I think he kind of looked at it as a fisherman's badge of honor or something like that.

It wouldn't be long and he'd have his life jacket back on with me on my new boat and hopefully we'd be catching a ton of fish then too. I knew we didn't have many trips together like that left because I wouldn't be around much longer. I wasn't sure how he'd handle me being away but in truth, I didn't know how I was going to handle it either. Sammy wasn't just my brother, he was my best friend. He made me and even Jacob better people, that is, all except towards each other.

So many outsiders thought Sammy was the one with the problems but it was never him it all. He was just like John Lennon said and more so of how we all should have been more often. He was happy and he was happy all of time. Our childhood was filled with many things. Some of it was what many would consider bad but for us, it was mostly wonderful. Life sometimes didn't feel easy but my parents always made it work. Most of the time they seemed to make it work well and with Sammy around, it was often a lot of fun too.

Spring Has Sprung

When fishing season arrived, I, as promised, made plans to take Sammy on the maiden voyage. I told him that it was bad luck for a boat not to have a name so I was going to bestow the honor upon him to name our new floating fish slayer. He told me that he had to think about it for a while and he'd let me know. I wasn't expecting a delay in his decision for naming my boat but that's what happened. Anytime any of us thought we knew what Sammy was going to do or say, he'd often surprise us with something we never thought of. Along with a true happiness, he had a creativity that was simplistic but brilliant at the same time. In this case, this trait caused me to barely be able to wait to hear what he was going to name my boat.

I don't think either one of us slept a wink that night waiting for daybreak and our time to catch some of those beautiful fish. We just knew they were waiting for us with open mouths, especially now that we had a boat to seek them out from. We had the life jackets, worms, fishing poles and boat all loaded up and ready to go. At what I thought was the perfect time, we left out on our first adventure in my new boat. My mother always made Sammy ride in the back seat even when he was older but because I had an old pickup truck, there was no back seat.

He always seemed a little nervous sitting in the front and when Sammy got nervous, he talked a lot—even more than usual. Everything we drove past, he'd quickly relate to fishing and some other aspect of his life. I felt like I was listening to one of the great philosophers of the past as I just drove and listened while daring not to interrupt this young Einstein. When we arrived at the loading ramp, Sammy got out to direct me into the water. I think he forgot his duties, however, because all he wanted to do was stand by the pier and greet everyone that was around with a "Good day." After launching the boat, I realized that I had forgotten the oars.

A Jon boat doesn't have a gas motor and I didn't have a trolling motor at the time, so the only way we could really go anywhere was by rowing it the best we could with our hands. So basically, because of my forgetfulness, we could only get as far as where we usually fished from on the bank. At first, I thought about going back home to get the oars but unlike usual, Sammy had his line in the water first and almost as soon as we left the dock. His rod was bouncing back and forth and all over the place almost as soon as his bait hit the water with the first fish of the day on the end of it. His eyes lit up even more than usual as he started telling me how to fish from that point on.

He was now not only the first one to catch a fish but he was evidentially also a professional fisherman and fishing tour guide as well. I did reluctantly listened to his guidance, however, because his knowledge was proven when my rod started jerking back and forth also. We caught so many fish that day not even twenty feet from where we usually fished on dry land from. It must have been something about being in a boat because we'd never caught that many fish on the shore before and especially not as many of those greatly desired bass and catfish as we did that day.

After about an hour of pulling in one fish after another, it began to drizzle. I asked Sammy if he wanted to go home and I guess since we were catching so many fish, he said, "No way, I'm killin 'em." Of course, that wasn't a literal statement because he still made me throw all of them back as usual, but we did catch a lot of fish that day. The drizzle became a rain, then almost a downpour but Sammy dared me to move the boat an inch until the fish stopped biting. The more it rained, the more fish we caught. I noticed that my feet were getting wet but not directly from the rain. It seemed to be coming from the bottom up. When I looked down, I saw that water puddles were collecting throughout the boat and especially around my feet. I had a Big Gulp cup so I began to scoop it out as fast as I could.

After my second or third scoop Sammy yelled out, "I got it!" I thought he caught another fish but that wasn't what he was talking about. Out of nowhere, he said he had come up with a name for my new boat. Sammy wasn't worried at all about how it was raining so hard that the boat was filling up as fast as I could scoop it out. He had named my boat and wanted me to know what he came up with right then. Sammy yelled out, "*Puddles!*" I think in the maritime history of boats I doubt very seriously that any boat has ever been named *Puddles* before, but it was definitely fitting. His name for the boat was so obvious and simple yet so creative at the same time. I didn't want the boat to live up to its name too much that day. We both laughed at the very fitting name and began to pack up for the long, twenty-foot hand paddle back to the dock.

It took about ten times as long to get back to the dock as it would have with oars but Sammy enjoyed the wet ride and he was very proud of the clever name that he came up with for my boat. Since the clouds were darker and more fluid than usual, he was also enjoying the sky boobies that he claimed he saw and let me proudly know were moving around at a much faster pace than on most days.

When we finally made it home, similarly to how he excitedly told everyone about his time at Disney World, he did the same about our day of fishing. He was proven to be a true fisherman too because every time he told someone about his day, the waves, the fish, the puddles and even the sky boobies got bigger and bigger. Before long, he was speaking as if he had caught Moby Dick the wale from the deck of the Titanic right before it sank due to an iceberg but also because of those many puddles. It was a great day with a great kid. I'm not so sure that I would have ever been appreciative enough towards him if he wasn't like he was. I know that's not saying much about me but Sammy really was the greatest blessing in my life and regardless of the reasons, I never took him for granted and always greatly enjoyed my time with him.

Puddles

My graduation time had finally arrived. There were many times that I didn't think I'd make it that far, but I did. I think even Jacob was happy for me, possibly for no other reason than I'd finally be leaving the house at the end of the summer. On my graduation day everyone dressed up in their Sunday best and made their way to the high school auditorium for the event. Sammy had a little bow tie with the word *graduate* on it in my honor, and with graduation being at the high school, he was very comfortable being there.

He was so comfortable that when the principal asked him to be the school's graduation greeter he had absolutely no problems with it all and welcomed everyone with a continuously open mouth himself. He sat at the entrance and must have said, "Good day," five hundred times, greeting everyone who arrived in his comical but ever so special way. When all the graduates sat down and he had welcomed each and every one of the visitors who came to graduation, he then came and sat down right beside me instead of sitting in the stands like everyone else who wasn't graduating that day. Nobody minded and I was honored to have my best friend sit right next to me on the day of my greatest accomplishment thus far in my life.

When they called my name to receive my diploma, I think Sammy was happier than I was. He got up on his chair and cheered and screamed and even ran down and met me at the foot of the steps as I was getting off of the stage. The whole auditorium rose to their feet and cheered with him. I knew it wasn't for me but that made me even more proud to graduate in such a way. Later that night, Sammy's mood turned to something quite the opposite. I knew he realized I'd be leaving soon but I don't think it fully hit him until after we got back home that night. The one thing Sammy always had trouble with was the concept of time. I was leaving but not for two more months, so we still had time to go on many more adventures, do a few more art projects and go on a few more fishing trips.

Once I let him know that, he didn't need to hear anything else because that was enough to change his mood back to where it was earlier in the auditorium. At the time, whether you call this using him or not, and even though it wasn't meant that way, Jacob and I taught Sammy how to go up to the cutest girls in our school and flirt with them. One of his philandering trips gained me my first real girlfriend, Abbey, and like most people, I think she liked Sammy more than she did me. I didn't really mind though because I did too.

She was a very nice girl and would often come over to play Uno or Yahtzee with us. I think Sammy had a little crush on her too so we often took him with us when we went places. The day after graduation, Abbey was going to the SPCA to pick out a new puppy. I knew for a fact that Sammy would love that so we took him along with us. I always knew Sammy had a nurturing, even healing side to him. He always took such care of everything he touched, especially animals. When we walked into that kennel, regardless of all of the barking that was going on in efforts to gain our attention, he walked by each and every cage, one by one, to spend a little time with every dog so none felt left out. The dogs actually seemed to calm down quite a bit when Sammy said whatever it was, he was saying to them.

I thought I was watching the dog whisperer but then I just remembered—no, it's just my brother, my very, very special brother. Abbey finally picked out the dog that she wanted and called Sammy over to get his seemingly all-knowing approval. I think Sammy thought he still had to flirt with her because he winked at Abbey, as to say, "That's the one, babe." Abbey giggled and off we went—me, Abbey, Abbey's new puppy and the newly-crowned dog whisperer. We took it back to our house to play with it some and Sammy was so good and loving with the dog that it gave me an idea.

The only problem was, it was an idea that I would need to get approval on before ever enacting. We never had a pet before but after seeing Sammy at that kennel, I knew Sammy would definitely give any animal everything it could ever need. After I told my mother how Sammy reacted when he thought I'd be leaving after my graduation and how he was at the kennel I don't think she had any other choice than to say yes to my planned departing gift. We had a few more adventures and we went out on a few more fishing trips. On those, I made sure I didn't forget the oars but before long, it was time for me to get ready to actually leave. I didn't really talk to Sammy about it too much because I didn't want him to be sad and I really didn't want to be sad myself either.

Now, ready or not, it was time and I asked him if he wanted to go back to where Abbey got her puppy from. He could hardly say yes fast enough. During this trip in my truck, in the front seat, all of his conversations were about dogs. When we got back to the kennel, before we went in, I told him that I wanted to talk to him for a minute. He was excited to go in but he also at least pretended like he wanted to hear what I had to say. I told him that I'd be leaving soon for college. Once again, his face dropped in sadness but I also told him that I talked our mother and she said he could have a puppy, more or less in my place.

Whenever he missed me, he had a buddy himself to help in making it a bit easier on him. I was a little hurt because he definitely heard that he could have a puppy and jumped out of the truck and rushed in the kennel doors as if I already said all that he needed to know. As he looked through the dog enclosures, he was even more involved this time. He took all of the time that he needed to pick out just the right one. I don't think any of those dogs realized how blessed they'd be if they were the one that Sammy picked but as he got to a cage of one of the scruffier looking puppies in it, I tried to keep him moving. He wasn't having any of it. He had to give that little guy an equal chance too. As Sammy held that previously unwanted puppy, the dog started peeing on him.

I knew Sammy would move on then, especially after I yelled out, "Yuck!" Sammy didn't though. He picked that little pee-er up and once again winked but this time it was at me as to make the signal that he had finally made his choice. I've learned not to doubt any of Sammy's decisions so this time it was me, Sammy and the lucky little pee-er on the way home. Sammy was happy after fishing, he was definitely happy after returning home from Disney World.

In truth, Sammy was happy all of the time but I've never seen him as happy as he was with his new puppy.

This time he didn't have to take any time to name it either. He knew his name from the minute that dog sprinkled all over him. Sammy introduced me and everyone else to Puddles, his new dog. With a boat and a dog named Puddles, there was no way to forget either one of them now.

College-Bound

Sammy, in his own way, was relating everything we did together to the names that he chose and I loved both of the names that he selected, even if they were the same. By this time, Jacob and I had for the most part been doing our own thing for quite a while, but for one last time before I left, I planned to take both of my brothers out to the field down the street from our house to cloud gaze one last time. This time, we'd have to take Puddles the dog with us, but since Sammy had very much made him an equal part of our family almost from the second, he brought him home, that was more than fine with me. While we were lying there, Sammy didn't call out a single booby that day. He was seeing things like dog bones and dog toys more so than anything else.

I knew for once I had made a good decision in helping him find something that would be very important to him, but also something else that he could take care of like he did with me without him even realizing how much he actually did. Jacob and I were on common ground under the sky, looking at those clouds so he basically wished me well, and because Sammy didn't do it, he called out the booby sightings for the group. Sammy may not have found them himself, but he and I still laughed every time Jacob did, just like immature seven year-olds would have.

That night, I packed up all of my stuff in the back of my old truck and put a tarp over it to be ready to leave the next morning. As I was packing, I looked up in the window and saw Sammy looking at me through the window once again. Just like the time when mom locked us out of the house, I knew Sammy was going to miss me and I definitely knew I was going to miss him right back. As Sammy was waving, I saw Puddles jump up and lick him on the side of his cheek. I thought to myself, *Puddles is doing his job as planned*, and I finished loading up. When morning came, I left early and purposefully before anyone else woke up. I had already said my goodbyes and I didn't want my going to college being any sadder than it already was, besides, I didn't want Jacob to throw a party that early in the morning either.

On the six-hour drive to my new college at West Virginia University, I thought back about how Jacob and I always fought but also about how in such contrast Sammy and I always enjoyed each other so much. I still didn't know how the same blood line could be so different, but it always was. I also thought about how appreciative I was that my parents gave up so much of their own lives so we could have the lives that we did. I knew I had to do better in college than I did in high school where I barely got by.

I never had trouble with school, I just didn't see where it helped but so much either. I was the first one in our family to ever go to college and I felt I had to do it for them as much as for myself. Besides, if for no other reason than since I graduated high school first, this would be something that Jacob couldn't beat me at. That was, of course, if I did what I was supposed to do. Once there, I realized college was very much like high school except the classes were bigger and my life was more expensive. I didn't realize until then that I took so many things for granted back at home. Things like toilet paper and food were so expensive that when I wasn't at school, I had to work all of the time myself. I really didn't have time to do anything else, but I was bound and determined to make it work.

Regardless of my busyness, I did make sure I was around on Sunday evenings because that was the time that either I called my family or my family called me. Everyone, to include Sammy, seemed to be fine with me being gone and besides, puddles was there to take my place. Most of the first semester roared by and before I knew it, it was time for spring break. Now, the rich kids may have been going to Daytona Beach or Mexico or somewhere else exotic like that but us working class students were going home. Other than not being able to afford to go anywhere else, I wanted to go home anyway.

I knew I missed my parents, Sammy and maybe even Jacob a little. I even missed both of the Puddles—the dog and my boat—so I headed home at the very second my last class was over. On the long drive back, a certain peace came over me that Sammy and the rest of my family seemed to handle my being away without any issues. I felt this was the way things were supposed to be. Everyone seemed to be getting on with their lives fine, to include me. Regardless of our newly settled lives, I was still grateful and excited to be going back home to visit for a while and I hoped they were just as excited with me coming as well.

Armageddon

When I got home, it was as if I just got back from a war or something like that because everyone was so happy to see me. Believe it or not, I even think Jacob missed me. My parents even both shockingly took a day off from work that week too. What overwhelmed me the most was Jacob said that he wanted to go fishing when Sammy and I went. I told him it was alright if he didn't go because I knew he really didn't like to fish, but he insisted. I knew it was supposed to be drizzling again around the end of the week and remembering back to how many fish Sammy and I caught on our last rainy trip, I thought we could duplicate our efforts under similar circumstances.

Like life seems to do, that week flew by and Saturday, our fishing day, was soon upon us. For the first time, Jacob and Puddles would be joining us. When we got to the dock, Sammy jumped out for his multiple rounds of "Good days" once again and this time Jacob actually helped me back the boat into the water. I also managed not only to bring the oars this time but also an electric trolling motor that I bought secondhand from that old nosey neighbor. My plan was to roam the river until everyone caught a bunch of fish. Anyway, as expected, the rain for whatever reason brought the fish in once again and this time, with Jacob there, it looked like we'd catch even more than Sammy and I did before.

Once the fish took a break in one place, I cranked up that little electric motor and chased them down again. My plan was working perfectly and we were all acting like brothers more so than we probably ever did in our lives. I also think what helped was, we were catching so many fish that we didn't have time to worry about anything else. I know if Puddles the dog could have held a rod even he would have caught plenty of fish that day. Once our arms became sore from all of the reeling, we headed back in. That entire day there was a large boat racing back and forth across the river. I noticed it at first because of its size and speed, but later because of its name.

Sammy named my little boat *Puddles* because of the rain water that accumulated around my feet during the last extremely rainy fishing trip but I had no idea why that big boat was named *The Armageddon*. It wasn't necessarily following us, it was just so big and fast that when it sped around the river, it seemed to be everywhere all at once. Now, a trolling motor is a lot better than paddling— especially with your hands—when you forget your oars, but it isn't fast at all either. As we putted towards the dock to put the boat up for the day, that huge boat was headed right for us and its driver didn't even realize it.

Jacob started screaming and both of us tried to grab Sammy and Puddles to help them jump to safety, but neither of us could get to them in time. *The Armageddon* completely ran over my little Jon boat and all of us who were inside of it too. It threw me under the water for what seemed like forever, but when I finally resurfaced, I saw Puddles and Jacob swimming towards the shore but I didn't see Sammy anywhere. My heart sank. I knew Sammy had a life jacket on but I didn't know if that huge boat's propeller tore him to pieces or even where he was at all. Jacob and I screamed out over and over again but Sammy was nowhere to be found. Terror set in as the man in the big boat realized what he had done and turned back around to check on his negligence. As he drove that boat next to me, some older tan shirtless guy pulled me in.

I could barely get the words out that my little brother that he just carelessly ran over was missing. Before I had a chance to say a word, the man that was driving the boat pointed at something in the water. What would have taken me almost an hour to get to in my boat took him only a minute to arrive at. It was Sammy and he was face down in the water, covered in blood. I jumped back in the river again to get what I thought was just the body of my little brother as fast and fearfully as I could.

When I rolled him over he wasn't breathing. I quickly handed Sammy's lifeless body up to the men in the boat. The shirtless man performed CPR on him and thank God he began spitting up water and breathing again. As he sputtered up the water that had settled in his lungs, it was plain to see that he was still very much hurt and slashed in several places. He needed to get to the hospital as quickly as possible. Jacob, in his fear and caring, had already called the police and rescue squad from the shore and they were practically waiting for us at the dock when we got there. The rescue team snatched Sammy from the big boat at the dock and directed us to meet them at St. Mary's hospital as soon as we could. As the ambulance sped off, Jacob, myself and Puddles hurried to my truck as fast as we could to head to St. Mary's ourselves where my poor little hurt brother was headed.

St. Mary's

J acob also wisely called our mother at work to tell her what had happened. I know that had to have been a terrible call but she and my father had to be on the way to the hospital themselves by now. Almost as soon as we got into my truck, Jacob started screaming at me. I didn't respond because I felt that I deserved it even though I didn't see any of the events of that day coming or how I could have stopped them. He asked me why I ever had to come back home. I simply drove without saying a word because I was asking myself the exact same question in my own mind. I knew he was scared that Sammy was really hurt, but for now, at a minimum we knew he was breathing.

As I drove, I kept thinking back to the time that our mother locked us out of the house and I remembered her absolute disappointment in us. To me, it was the worst punishment that she ever issued. This time I wasn't worried about getting in trouble, I was just praying that Sammy was going to be okay. It was my responsibility to make sure he was and I did the opposite of that on the river that day. As we pulled into the emergency room parking lot, both of my parents' cars were already there and they were both already inside. Jacob jumped out and ran inside himself but I didn't.

For the first time that I can remember, I prayed as hard as I could. I prayed for my brother so much on my deliberately unhurried way in. As I walked in the hospital, my mother and father ran up to me as I'm sure they did to Jacob when he came in also. They didn't seem to blame me, but it didn't matter. I blamed myself enough. Sammy was back in surgery for what we later found out was a broken arm and some other pretty serious lacerations. Other than that, thank God he was going to be okay. He would definitely have scars from that day but I knew that I would too. The thing about my parents was, even though they always treated Sammy the same, they knew he wasn't. They knew in many ways his life was more delicate than others and all of us had to protect and appreciate it a bit more. I really thought I had done that up until that point.

When Sammy was discharged, Jacob wouldn't ride home with me. I know he knew that I couldn't help what happened, but either way, it happened and it could have killed Sammy. That night, being that I was in the attic in a space directly above my parents' room, I overheard them talking. They didn't blame me in what they thought was their private conversation but they did talk about how scared they were and their need to protect Sammy even more—even if it was from me, his oldest brother. I honestly felt that, not only did I let Sammy down, but I also let my parents down once again.

I was supposed to look out for him no matter what, and regardless of the situation, I didn't. What made matters much worse was, all through the night I heard my mother sob about what could have been. You can call it shame or self-disappointment or even cowardice but I just couldn't bear to look them in the eye the next morning after what had happened. I left an apology letter for everyone, to include both of my brothers, and headed back to school in the middle of the night. I don't know what I would have done if that fishing trip would have killed my beloved brother. I took all of the precautions, I did everything I knew how to do, but it wasn't enough to protect him as he should have been protected. I was so thankful that Sammy would be okay, but I wasn't so sure that I would be.

My insides were still jittery with fear and shame during the whole ride back to college. The next day, my mother called about four or five times but I never answered. I didn't call her back either. I was so sad that once again I had disappointed my family and I didn't want to speak to anyone. This overwhelming guilt went on for over a month. During that whole time, I don't think I slept for more than a couple hours a night. My grades almost dropped to the point where I was in danger of failing out of school. Once I realized it, I scheduled an appointment with my academic advisor.

When I met with her, she suggested a study abroad program for the summer to try and boost up my GPA. I knew if I went, I could not only make up for my academic shortcomings, but I also wouldn't have to go back home for the summer. I talked to my family some after that original avoidance, but it was never on a regular basis like it was before. Sammy healed and definitely didn't blame me or hold any grudges. Just like with the life jacket, I think he looked at his new scars as another fisherman's badge of honor. I was still his big buddy, but it almost hurt too much to hear his voice. I was the one who took him to the place where he almost lost his life. I really did believe that Jacob was right and everyone would be better off if I just stayed away.

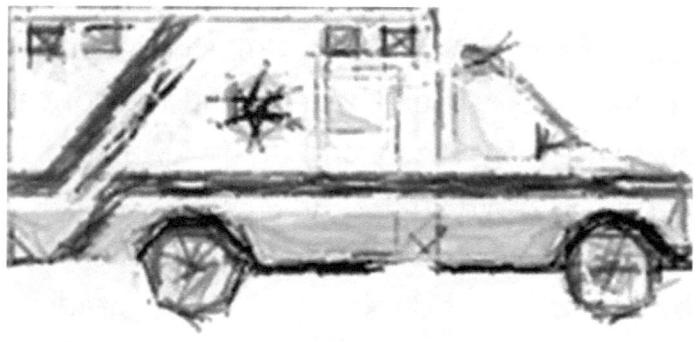

Israel Goes to Israel

I was at school to get an art degree. Sammy and I piddled around with painting and sculpturing and things like so much that we eventually got to the point where we were both pretty good at it. I never thought I'd go to college, especially not on a partial scholarship for art, but I did. Now, to save my academic standings, I had to go to another country for the whole summer according to my advisor. As irony would have it, that other country was Israel. All I could do was shake my head because apparently Israel was going to Israel. I missed my family but I really did think it was best if I was somewhere else for a while longer. I went as far away as I could think of, even though I never thought of it myself. Life works that way sometimes. When everything seems like it's finally working out, it changes for some reason.

This change had me going to Israel with two other guys who were also art students. I can't say that I seemed to fully relate to them at first because I was never what most other art students at our school chose to look like. I didn't have earrings or tattoos, or even a non-traditional haircut. I think I looked more like a straight-laced ignoramus than the rest of the students in my program or the ones on the trip with me did, but regardless of our comparisons, off to the holy land we went.

When we arrived at Ben Gurion, Israel's national airport, we could definitely tell this wasn't like anywhere any of us had been ever been before. The first thing I noticed was there was an extreme amount of security. The United States greatly enhanced airport security after 9/11, but it was nothing like it was there. A security officer approached our little group and started asking what seemed like a million questions. The main one's he wanted definite answered to were, what business we had in the country and where we were staying. After we told him that we were art students studying abroad and showed him our credentials to prove it, we gave him the name and address of our hotel in Jerusalem.

We were staying at the Waldorf Astoria about forty-five minutes away. I came from a very working class family, so I never dreamed about staying anywhere like the Waldorf Astoria in any country, but after what seemed like an hour of interrogation, we were on our way to our summer palace. That place lived up to everything I imagined it would be and even more. The outside of the building had a Middle Eastern flair with huge sandy-colored stone bricks and windows that had that Arabian point at the top.

It was impressive and really big, but once inside, one of the first things that I noticed was there were wrought iron clocks on every wall representing all of the different languages of the world and the great diversity of their country. There was also a giant rotunda with a sky light at the top and nine floors of the most elegant rooms of any hotel that I've ever seen. I may have been running away in a sense but I ran to somewhere that was pretty nice. If there was anything negative about the place it was that we all had to share a room. I knew I wouldn't have any problem with that though because I've shared a room with two other guys the majority of my entire life.

The other guys didn't seem to mind it either, so there we all were, together at the Waldorf Astoria, smack dab in the middle of Jerusalem, Israel. The other student's names were Theodore and William. Sarcastically, once I got to know the young men a bit better, I often called them Bill and Ted after *Bill and Ted's Excellent Adventures*. Their nicknames seemed to stick and we all definitely hoped this would also be an excellent adventure in Israel. Back at our college, before I left, I submitted a painting that actually came in fifth place in a national art competition. The art from the top five students was advertised and used as collegiate promotional material throughout the country and probably the world as well.

It was an unexpected honor, but by the suggestion of my professor, I was to use the summer to figure out why my work didn't do better than fifth place. I thought that was a much better prize than I could have wished for but my professor didn't feel the same way. I know what happened to Sammy allowed me to pour my heart into that project, so I had no clue what that man could be talking about in regards to making it better. It was just another escape for me, but at the time, I really didn't know how to do more than I did, but I definitely knew that I didn't want any more motivation coming from any additional hurt family members, especially from Sammy.

The Holy Land

During our first week in Israel, we were pretty much were free to tour the country. The one thing to realize about Israel is it is very small. I think it's about the size of New Jersey and that's about it. We were able to see the majority of the most commonly visited places in the area, especially in the older part of Jerusalem during that first week. We saw the Dome of the Rock, the Sea of Galilee, the Mount of Olives, the Church of the Holy Sepulcher, where Jesus himself was crucified, and we even ate at a two-hundred year old café named Zalatimo's. They served these crispy little cheese desserts that none of us could get enough of. They were called Mutabaks and they were absolutely addictive.

Israel the country was very much like Israel the person, me. Both of us were filled with a great amount of confusion. The country was a definite representation of diversity but it seemed that the trait most commonly thought of as a positive feature with most things was a little more dangerous in its applications there. Walking down almost any street, we heard the English, Arabic and the Hebrew languages spoken. The people speaking them seemed to be making sure there wasn't any sort of a blending of the languages either. The varying cultures very much wanted everyone who visited to see their extremely vast differences and there were so many.

The old city of Jerusalem itself is divided into four quarters: the Muslim, Armenian, Jewish and Christian sections. They were all as different as night and day, and in certain areas, you really had to keep your eyes open for your own safety. My favorite destination in Israel was the Western Wall, otherwise known as the Wailing Wall. For some reason, that magnificent reminder of Israel's turbulent past also reminded me of home, and particularly, my brother Sammy. It was such a simple place but it gave so much hope to so many. Some came to give thanks and others were begging for hope, but either way, everyone who visited was permanently touched in some way.

The Wailing Wall really was such a simple place. It was nothing fancy but it had an absolute profoundness to it, just like Sammy did. For many, that wall is considered the holiest place on earth and we spent a lot of time there and at that old café eating those crispy treats while we were in the holiest of holy cities. The oldest part of Jerusalem, near where our magnificent hotel was, was no bigger than a few miles wide in any direction, so getting around to wherever we needed to go was fairly easy throughout the summer.

After the first week of sightseeing, we had to get to work. Even though we were all art majors, we still had to take core classes like everyone else, and just like everyone else, we rarely liked them. The art part of our education was usually somewhat enjoyable and this summer that is all we had to concentrate on. Each of us had an assigned project while there. Mine was to figure out how to make my submission from that competition better. Bill's was to rework a sculpture that he had been working on and Ted's had something to do with an abstract, something that I didn't come close to understanding.

Our classes were at Jerusalem University in the heart of that historic city and it was specifically located on Mt. Zion. Mt. Zion was the resting place of King David, the guy who killed Goliath in the Bible, so we had a lot to live up to in that city that seemed so surreal. Being that I had no idea how I would make my project any better, it took me a while longer than it did the others to get started. It's not that I didn't try or that it couldn't get better, I knew it could, but I just didn't know how to do it at the time.

Bill and Ted, unlike me, jumped right in to their work and often finished what they needed to for the day way before I ever even got started. Because of this, they often left me by myself staring at an easel without a clue of how I was going to make the stupid thing any better than what it was.

Let
THE
adventure
BEGIN

A 1970 Sussita

It was on one of those evenings alone that I kept feeling like I was being watched. I didn't see anyone around but I just felt like there was someone near. I looked around each classroom and down a few halls but I never found anyone. I just wrote it off to my imagination and returned to trying to figure out how to make that damn painting better. Another hour when by when I realized that I wasn't going to make any great breakthroughs that day so I decided to pack my stuff up and head back to the hotel. It was getting late and being that some of the areas that I had to walk through to get back to the hotel were a tad bit sketchy, I decided to take a bus back.

I waited for a ride at the bus stop for a while but nobody ever showed up. After waiting a few more minutes, I decided I would just walk back instead of waiting there all night without any guarantees of anyone ever coming. As I began walking, an old taxi pulled up beside me. The man inside the car asked me if I wanted a ride. There was already someone else in the back seat, but I had all of my supplies in my hands—to include that big easel—so I accepted his offer without a second thought. I'd seen similar cars like he had driving around during our time there but I didn't know what kind it was so, if for no other reason than to make small talk, I asked.

The man proudly told me we were riding in a 1970 Sussita. As he was telling me about how that particular model was the last to ever be made in Israel and other facts about his car, I tried to politely listen until I noticed that we were headed in the opposite direction of what I thought the Waldorf Astoria was in. I didn't say anything at first because I just figured he knew his country and its roads better than I did, so he had to know what he was doing. However, after we crossed a bridge that I knew I'd never seen before, I frantically asked him where we were going. That once nice man changed in an instant and pulled out a small hand gun, as did the man in the back seat.

At that point, my driver had one hand on the steering wheel while the other was on that gun pointed at my ribs. In the movies you always see the good guy knock the gun away from the bad guys and roll out the door to safety but in real life it simply isn't like that. I figured it wasn't a robbery because they would have done it long before then. I could only assume that they were going to take me somewhere to shoot me in the head or something like that for whatever reason. It may have just been because I was American. I simply didn't have a clue once again.

As we made our final turn down a long dirt road, I tried to at least pretend like I was in the movies and started to open the passenger door as quietly as I could in hopes of not being noticed. That old door squeaked so loudly that as soon as I tried to open it, the gun that was once pointed at my side was now raised and pointed at my head. To confirm their control of the situation, the man in back seat followed suite as well. I knew then, with two guns pointed at my head, I was doomed to follow whatever directions that were given to me. As we reached the end of that bumpy dirt road, we stopped at an old factory. It looked like it had been out of business for as long as Israel had been out of the automobile industry.

As we stopped, the driver directed me to stay in the car and the man in the back seat still made sure that his gun was pointed at my head just in case I had any other bright ideas. The man that disappeared in the building wasn't gone long, but when he did return, it was my turn to go inside. When the two men walked me into that old dilapidated building, the main thing I noticed was it smelled like death itself. It must have been some kind of old meat processing plant or something like that in its past because the stench was so pungently abusive. After we were inside, the man who had been driving led me into what must have been an old meat locker. He forced me into that pitch-black metal cooler and slammed the door shut.

I then heard what must have been chains being wrapped around the handle outside the door, and soon after, a click from a padlock closing. It was pitch-black in my makeshift prison and the slime from whatever was in there before I was inhabited every square inch of that nasty place. I couldn't see anything, so I felt my way around until I found the driest area to sit down and try to figure out if there was anything at all that I could do to get out of that very unexpected and terribly smelly prison cell that those men just put me in.

Meat Locker

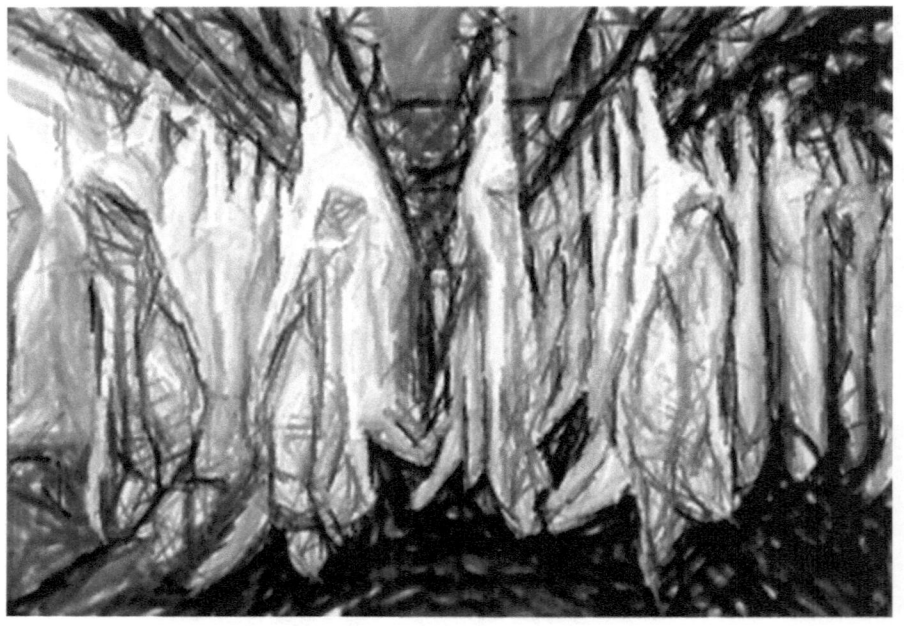

What I'm guessing to be about an hour went by, and since I didn't hear anything from outside of that meat locker anymore, I got up and slammed my shoulder against the door a few times in hopes of getting out. That thick, insulated metal door didn't budge. I rammed it over and over again if for no other reason than to give my mind something to do, because for the life of me, I never expected to get kidnapped in a foreign country. I could see possibly getting stabbed or maybe even shot, but not kidnapped.

I almost laughed thinking about if my capturers wanted a ransom, they definitely picked the wrong person. There was no way that was going to happen because my parents didn't have any money and I didn't either. I was just a poor student studying abroad, nothing more and nothing less. After I failed at even coming close to busting through that door, what felt like another hour passed and once again I heard voices. This time, it was arguing; it sounded a lot like the rants that Jacob and I used to have. One man had the definite upper hand and seemed to be strongly questioning the other about something. I could barely hear their heated conversation through the thick walls of that cooler but I was trying to as hard as I could because I was sure whatever it was they were arguing about had something to do with me.

I thought, now at least at a minimum I'd find out what their intentions with me were. As the chains once again rattled, the lock also clicked once more, but this time it was to let me out instead of to hold me in. The same man who stole me in the first place grabbed me by the arm and led me down a long carpeted hall. I didn't see a gun this time but I obviously remembered he had one. The further we went through that giant building, the nicer the carpet got and the less abandoned the building looked as well. That building was absolutely huge so we walked for a while, and the more we did, the more accommodating the building became.

When we reached our intended destination, it looked more like a modern-day office more so than anything else. There was a conference table and chairs, a white board and even a computer and a phone in the room. The man who led me there didn't say a word until we arrived at the room, he put me in, and then all he said then was, "Sit down." I think he was the one who was just scolded by whoever else it was outside of the cooler before they let me out. The reason I thought that way was because of the flushed look on his face. That's a look I'm sure I had a thousand times on my own face when Jacob would hit himself and then hide in the closet so I'd get a whipping.

That man may not have gotten a beating, but he definitely lost an argument and it showed heavily on his face.

As I sat there by myself for a few minutes, another man entered and closed the door behind him. This guy looked nothing like the taxi driver who brought me there. The taxi driver was middle age and kind of frumpy with salt-and-pepper-colored hair and so was the man from the back seat. This new man was well-dressed, well-groomed and he had a very distinctive look about him. He was definitely of Middle Eastern decent but he spoke without any sort of accent at all. He seemed genuinely concerned about how I was so abruptly brought to that old building and especially how I was thrown in that meat locker at gun point for the past few hours.

Things just weren't adding up. This man looked to have more money than I'd ever have, so I doubted he wanted any type of ransom—as if it could be paid anyway. I was also almost sure that if any of them just wanted to rob me or even kill me, they surely would have done it before then. None of this made any sort of sense to me at all. As he sat down at the table where I was already sitting, the original two men also came back in, and this time, instead of carrying guns, they had some of those cheesy Mutabaks and coffee from Zalatimo's with them. This kidnapping now seemed to turn into some kind of civil business meeting that evidentially included snacks, and one that I was very much forced to attend.

Conference Room Snacks

Regardless of his politeness, I had an overwhelming feeling that the well-dressed man whom was now talking directly to me was a lot of things, but I doubted very seriously that any of them included being a legitimate business man. He was courteous but I could tell that he absolutely got what he wanted, and when he wanted it, too. As we sat there, there wasn't a great deal of beating around the bush on his part. He told me that he saw my painting on the internet and he wanted me to paint something very similar for his son. I about fell out of my seat. I almost even laughed because I was far from a professional artist. I was just a college student in a foreign country who, for the most part, was already failing at what I was assigned to do, and his demand was virtually the same thing.

I still just knew he had to have me mixed up with someone else, and besides, why did he have his men kidnap me to get me to do something I probably would have at least tried if he would have just asked? As he spoke, however, he definitely had an urgency to his request. It seemed I had to do what he asked me to and I had to do it right then. The two men from before brought my original painting in and set it up on an old easel in the corner of the room. They also brought in the rest of my supplies and a fresh canvas.

My idea at that point was just to give him my other painting and hopefully that would be enough for him to let me go and get the hell out of there, but again, that's not what he wanted. This request was so strange it was almost comical, but the funniness ended when I remembered the two guns that were pointed at my head earlier that day. This man was so confusingly serious. I originally poured my heart into my first painting because of what happened to Sammy. I had so much guilt that it had to be released in some way, and for me, it was in that original painting.

I realized that I really couldn't do anything about The Armageddon running us over or really what happened to Sammy at all, but I couldn't help it. I had to get what could have happened out of my mind, and that time, I chose to paint my feelings away. When I think about how we almost lost my brother, it was just too much for me to handle. That painting and the way I threw myself into it was my only relief. My parents and even Sammy himself didn't blame me at all, but I blamed myself enough for everyone, and in truth, I still wasn't fully over it. Me being in Israel in the first place was my continued effort in trying to heal in a way but it was also me being too weak to face my issues and go home.

When my professor noticed there could be more in my painting, without acknowledging that he was telling the truth, I fully knew what he was talking about. I absolutely knew what he meant. As I poured my heart into that painting, all of my emotions were applied and I think the competition judges saw the love and compassion that was definitely there but my professor actually saw the anger and pain. I was secretly glad that I wasn't overly rewarded for that part of my work. That was the part that was so apparent to my professor, even if to no one else. The problem was, what this man wanted from me now was what I'd had so much trouble figuring out at Jerusalem University during the week. Now it appeared that I had an armed deadline and would have to figure something out either way.

Before I started, I guess he noticed me looking at the phone. He openly assured me that it worked but also clearly told me not to use it. My original thoughts were, if I ever got a moment by myself, I'd try to call for help. The problem was, I didn't know if Israel had something like 911 or not and I really didn't know who I could call for help anyway. I got my wish though because it appeared the men were going to lock me in the room until I completed their request by myself.

Painting isn't something you can just do in an hour or two, or even much more sometimes. There are layers after layers that have to be applied. I knew the last one took me about 30 straight hours and I just felt this one would take much longer—mainly because, once again, I didn't have a clue where to start. In the first painting I felt like every emotion that I was experiencing had to be put on, brush stroke by brush stroke, with such care—like I should have given to Sammy. I honesty felt in many ways I was painting it for him as much as for myself or any other reason. Each color reflected a different feeling that I was having at the time.

I thought to myself, how could I paint on demand? I wasn't a professional artist. I was barely still a student, but regardless of any of my wandering thoughts, I readied the canvas and spread out my brushes and acrylics if for no other reason but to pretend like I knew what I was going to do. As I dipped my brush into the paint, I began about two thirds of the way up the canvas. I chose to use the darkest colors for an outline, still not knowing where my attempts at painting this time would go. I've always loved looking up at the sky with my brothers and I really enjoyed painting it, too, so I decided to start there with a cerulean blue. That was not only my favorite color but my favorite shade of any color also.

Cerulean blue is almost as beautiful as the sky itself and as I spread that magnificent color from corner to corner. I couldn't get my mind off of that phone that I was dared not to use. Quietly, seeing that no one was around, I stepped over to it knowing that I had to dial 1-0-0 before reaching the United States and then I dialed my parent's number. I knew if anyone could help me, they could. The phone rang about four times. At first, I thought that no one was at home and I'd have to leave a message telling them that I'd been kidnapped in Israel.

I could only imagine how that message would be taken, and even though I knew that would greatly upset them, I felt that would be the only thing I could do with such few other options in play. As I was getting ready to leave such a terrible message, in the nick of time I all of a sudden heard a very much missed voice at the other end say, "Good day." It was Sammy and he was so excited to hear from me as well. I kept trying to ask him to get our mother or father but in all of his excitement he just kept talking over me. He told me about Puddles and Jacob and even told me about how his scars had healed so well. He told me about our parents even though he wouldn't let me talk to them.

Sammy got so many words in our—or should I say, his conversation—in (even though it couldn't have lasted more than three minutes) before the two men who were armed the day before, and probably also then, came back in the room and ripped the phone out of my hand and out of the wall too. I tried to get help, but after they yelled at me for a while, it really looked like I was really going to have to paint something for real now. As I put the brush back in my hand, I thought about Sammy's voice that I just heard for the first time in a while. When I did, a smile came over my face and my heart, too.

His voice, even though it was only for a very few minutes, gave me any and all of the inspiration I'd ever need. Just like before, bit by bit, I started building colors on top of colors until before I knew it, slowly but surely, a rough outline of an amazing landscape was developing. Little by little, the more I thought about my middle brother, the more that painting came to life. I knew the men were outside the door sitting in fold out chairs, now making sure I didn't do anything but paint, but I didn't care because I wanted to paint. Even greater than the last, the new painting began to come together with ease and without anger, even though I was forced to paint it. It still wasn't a fast process, but by the next morning, I was finished.

I painted throughout the night without realizing any time went by at all. This time, unlike the last, I could tell this one was special. It's as if God himself gave me the sights straight from his eyes and the thoughts from his breath to add a sky scene here, and a river and its surroundings there. As the man who made me paint the picture came back in, he saw what God blessed us with as well. He sat down at the table and placed his head in his hands as if to try to hold back his tears. He profusely apologized once again for making me paint in such a way and assured me that he'd take me back to the university that his henchmen grabbed me from very soon.

He told me he'd be back in an hour or so and then we would leave, and this particular excellent and very unexpected adventure would be concluded at that time. As he left, he also told his two men to bring in more of those treats and coffee for us to indulge in until he got back. The men who just yesterday threw me into an old, disgusting meat locker were now sitting at the table with me, eating snacks and drinking coffee like we were old friends. I was cordial but in no way was I trusting to anyone related to this strange yet surprisingly productive situation.

A Blessing in Common

After a strong hour passed, the man in charge of that crazy day and a half returned. When he did, he also brought in a young man in a wheel chair with him. This young man was probably just a few years younger than me, maybe Sammy or even Jacob's age. I could definitely tell that he was very sick from something. I never asked what was wrong with him, but when the young man saw the painting that I had just finished, he struggled to roll himself over to it. He eventually labored his way across the room to where it was on his own. He had that same look in his eyes; that look of gratitude that Sammy always had. It wasn't the man who wanted my painting, it was his sick son. It's not that this made the situation make any more sense, it's just now the reasoning didn't matter as much.

I realized then myself that me and that well-dressed man had something—or should I say, someone very much in common. I fully understood my blessed relationship with Sammy and how it would make me do almost anything to make him happy—or should I say, happier, even if it didn't make any sense at all to anyone else. My thoughts flooded towards my own brother and all of the struggles that he had, especially early in his life and more recently about our accident with *The Armageddon.*

This young man, also like Sammy after I pulled him from the river that day, was very pale, but unlike Sammy, he had an oxygen tube draped around his shoulders and back and attached to his nose. I didn't know how long he had but I knew without a shadow of a doubt that people who displayed illness like he did didn't have very long. His father was more than content with what I came up with for him but so much more than happy that his son was so satisfied with my efforts. As the man turned to me, he nodded and grinned in appreciation. He then signaled to the two men to take me out of the room. They quickly walked me out and back to that old Sussita that once again appeared to be my personal taxi.

As I got into car this time, the men let me sit in the back seat. I felt a little relief thinking that hopefully on this ride it at least wouldn't be at gunpoint. As we started pulling out, the grateful man from inside waved us down. He walked over to the car and handed me a large manila envelope. He gave me strict orders not to open it until later after I was dropped off. He genuinely thanked me once again for creating what I did for his son and once again apologized in true remorse for about the tenth time about how I was so abruptly taken there.

While driving back to the university, the men were talking as if nothing ever happened once again. The majority of their conversation towards me returned back to the driver's car and the weather. The men dropped me off near the university where I was taken, as if it was a real taxi ride as usual and wished me well and left as uneventfully as when they picked me up. I stood there dumbfounded at the past day and a half. I had no idea why any of that had to happen the way it did but there was a great deal of satisfaction in seeing the reaction in that sick young man's eyes to what God let me paint. I knew I couldn't take any real credit for that painting. I was just the vessel for a gift that would prove in the future to help so many through some of the toughest times in all of our lives.

In many ways that situation helped me as well. One reason was I wasn't going to have any more trouble completing my summer project. My assignment may not be as close to perfect as that painting was but it didn't matter. That painting made me realize where the real beauty comes from. Another reason was because when I opened that big manila envelope that the well-dressed man gave me, I could only gasp because there was $10,000 in cash inside of it and it was all in crisp, new one-hundred dollar bills.

The man, out of his extreme gratitude, gave me an amount that I'd never seen before. I never had money like that and I doubt very seriously that my parents ever had either. I knew with such a great financial blessing, I couldn't waste it. I had to use it for something that would actually help my parents in some way. They always gave so much to us and I felt that I had to figure out how this blessing could also bless them in some substantial way. Instead of going directly back to the hotel, I went back into the school and to my classroom. Bill and Ted were already inside working. They must not have missed me very much because they didn't say a word about me not going back to the room the night before.

I guess they probably thought I was just inspired by something and was just working through the night. If that's what they thought, they'd never know how right they were because that's exactly what happened just not in a way that anyone would ever expect or even know about. I decided to never tell my kidnapping story to anyone mainly because if for no other reason more good came from it than bad. The other good thing that came out of that day was after that I was able to leave early with my other two classmates as well. Since I also now had a handle on how to make my original painting so much better I had as much free time as they did and I used it too.

I then had time to visit even more of those beautiful places and we really did turn our trip into a most excellent adventure all the way around. The whole situation was strange and even scary at times but later, I'd learn how helpful my kidnapping was in so many ways, especially for some of the most important people in my life.

Old Gypsy Woman

We traveled throughout the country a little more and all three of us finished our assignments without issue. We greatly enjoyed each other's company and our ridiculously lavish accommodations. We also had many more of those cheesy Mutabaks and deeply rich Israeli coffees. I never told anyone who wasn't at that old building what happened, but there was one person that I didn't have to tell. A day before we left Israel, I was once again visiting the wailing wall. With it being my favorite place, I realized that I may never see it again in person so I wanted what it gave to everyone as much as I could get for myself for as long as I could. While admiring the appreciation that so many were showing and receiving from that holy place, an old gypsy woman walked up to me and grabbed me by the hand.

Having my money safely hidden in the room, I tried to tell the woman that I didn't have anything to give her but she didn't seem to care about getting paid. She took my hand in hers and turned it over as to get a closer inspection of my right palm. At first, I was mostly trying to be polite by letting her continue, but when she started telling me about the secret that I was trying to keep and almost all of the details about what happened to me in that old meat packing building, I have to admit, I was a little more than intrigued.

She described everything with such clarity and accuracy that the hair on the back of my neck stood up on its end. At first, I wondered if she was there herself because of how detailed her descriptions were about my experience, even the money. I thought, since she knew about the sum the well-dressed man gave me that she may have just been trying to scam me in some way to get to it, but that wasn't it. She never wanted a penny as she spoke about my past but also about what she claimed was going to be my future. Even though she didn't always use names, she spoke about how me and one of my siblings were at great odds. She also told me that I would have a very important decision to make about that rivalry.

One of the most frightful things she told me was I would have a great loss that would come into my life out of nowhere. The more she spoke, the worst things seemed to get and the more I wanted her to stop talking. I don't know why I didn't walk away but it was as if I was in a trance and couldn't pull my hand away from her if I wanted to. This creepy old lady told me I'd be in a great war where death itself would be the unfortunate and unexpected perennial theme of my life. She also told me that I'd eventually marry but not for too long. My life sounded like it was going to suck according to her.

One of the few positive things she did say was I'd have a daughter with beautiful, big, brown eyes and fluffy brown hair and she'd be the true love of my life. This old gypsy lady wouldn't let me go until she had fully told me everything that she wanted to. When she finally released my hand, I think I was more scared then than when I was kidnapped. Her words gave me nightmares for the next few days. The horrid images in my dreams of her words coming to fruition were so much clearer than anything that I could ever paint. That woman literally scared the hell out of me. Even when I got back to my college after the summer, her words had such a hold over me. I had no idea how she knew exactly what happened in the past but I prayed she was wrong about my future.

I tried to shake her words but I couldn't. I think if she didn't describe the past so clearly then I wouldn't have begun to believe what she had to say about what she so clearly described would be my future. For about two months there wasn't a time that at least once a day I didn't think about that old lady's words. They gave me an uneasiness and I didn't like it. I made my way through the rest of the next semester at school but I did so in fear. That lady implanted something in me that I just could not shake.

Not Him

When I finally made it back home for the next break, it didn't take long for me to realize that Sammy had been going back and forth to the doctor and had been doing so for quite a while without anyone telling me while I was away at school. The formal name for his heart problem was an atrioventricular septal defect, which basically meant he was born with these small holes in his heart. As he aged, his heart was pumping harder, but all of the things that his heart was supposed to control were slowing down. Sammy's doctor felt confident that with a small procedure he could mend much of his most pressing issues and Sammy would be as good as new in no time.

Sammy's heart operation was on a Monday and he only had to stay in the hospital for a day after it was successfully completed. Sammy acted as he always did—like it was no big deal, but with Sammy, everything really was a big deal. The Friday after his operation, after he'd been home for two days, Jacob and I got up and started our day. I can't ever remember a day growing up that we got up first. It was always Sammy waking us up. As I went into his room to wake up who I thought was just being a sleepy head, horror struck. Sammy wasn't sleeping and he wasn't breathing either. It appeared he hadn't taken a breath in a while. His beautiful body was already cold and stiff to the touch.

Puddles was lying beside him with his furry head on his shoulder. I'm sure that dog, in his own way, was also praying that he would just open his eyes once more and get up but that's not what happened. I screamed out for Jacob and when he ran in the room, he had the same reaction that I did just minutes before. Our beautiful brother was gone. We were crying and even Puddles seemed to have these huge alligator tears in his eyes as well. We all knew what we lost and we all realized how much we lost that morning, too. The greatest person I ever knew died in his sleep at the end of the very first week I got home after being away for so long.

Jacob and I both knew that call to our parents would almost be impossible to make but we still had to do it. This time I couldn't ask Jacob to do it for us, I had to make it myself. I had to at least act like the oldest brother one last time. There wasn't a part of me that wanted to tell my parents what had happened but I knew I had to. The best person by far that I have ever known was gone, my brother, but their son. My already broken heart crushed even more as I dialed my mother's work number and told her what had happened. She sobbed even more this time than ever before, but this time, it wasn't about any kind of disappointment in her oldest and youngest son. She sobbed as if God himself had let her down.

That was the only time in my life I dreaded my parents coming home from work. I knew having to see their hurt and pain would be absolutely terrible, but when they arrived, it was even worse than I could have imagined. They lost their son and most likely the greatest part of their hearts as well. Before the paramedics zipped Sammy's body up in that terrible body bag, I saw the scars that I helped create that day on the river. Those scars and his pitiful body would be a sight I'd never forget. I asked if Jacob and I could carry Sammy out ourselves to the awaiting ambulance. If nothing else, I wanted to do one last thing for him and that was all I could think of.

As Jacob and I carried Sammy out, we both looked up at the sky, a sky that had given us all such comfort so many times. This time, however, all we saw were scars. Those scars in the sky were from the gashes in our lives that had no way of ever fully healing. From that day forward, Sammy would be in that terrible sky. He would also be in our minds, hearts and constant thoughts forever. The brightest of bright lights burnt out way too early.

For the rest of my life I will always be able to hear his voice, feel his skin and know how much he blessed my life and the lives of my entire family. He was special, the most special person I ever knew.

Final Goodbye

One of the hardest things to do after a loved one dies is to go to the funeral home and pick out the casket, as well as deciding what words will go into their obituary. I realize it's very much a necessity but it's like pouring salt on a very fresh wound. When a death is so unexpected, it's even worse because, similar to a used car lot, you have to walk by the funeral home's casket samples that are so symmetrically laid out. Like when Sammy picked out Puddles, we had to look at each one and listen to why one was better than the other. The men who showed them to us were just doing their jobs, but the more they talked, the more we hurt.

This choosing was for our Sammy, and quite frankly, there had never been a casket made or words spoken that could come close to being good enough for him. Knowing that, my parents brokenheartedly did the best that they could in their selection. Everyone wants to give their loved ones the best final goodbye that they can. This may have been business as usual for the funeral home workers, but not for us. This was the final goodbye to the most important person in all of our lives. As the salesman calculated the cost of my brother's services, the price came out to be nine thousand nine hundred and ninety-nine dollars, and my parents wept once more.

This amount upset my mother. Not that she wouldn't have robbed a bank if she needed to for Sammy—she'd do anything to send off her son in the way she felt he deserved—it's just that she didn't have any idea how they'd realistically ever get that much money at once. If my mother was upset about the cost, my father was absolutely crushed and it wasn't totally about the price either. My parents didn't care about money, they never did. They just cared about us and providing for their boys. They both worked so much so we could have the life that we did—especially my father—but this time, my father felt like everything he had ever done didn't matter if he couldn't give Sammy what my mother wanted for him as a loving final farewell.

I overheard him tell my mother that he felt like a failure as he went over to the corner and appeared to be praying. After a few minutes, he came back across the room where we were and said, "I don't know where I'm going to get the money from yet, but for my boy, I will. Sign the papers for the amount and let's get out of here." From the minute I heard how much the funeral was, I knew what I was going to do, I just couldn't tell them. I knew they didn't have the money, but I also knew that I did, and if it was for Sammy and my parents, I couldn't have ever found a better place for it.

After we got back home, I snuck back out in my own truck, this time to pay the funeral home. My father was a lot of things; he was loving, he was kind and he was an extremely hard worker, but not a failure—not now and not ever. I made it extremely clear that I never wanted anyone to know where the money came from. I just wanted them to call my parents the second I left so that one worry could be taken off of their already extremely overfilled and extremely saddened plate. As I drove back home, thoughts of that old gypsy woman re-entered my mind. I yelled out at the air at her as if she was riding in the seat right beside me. I screamed, "Great loss? There is no greater!"

I knew then what she was talking about when she wouldn't let my hand go in Israel. I fully knew what my great loss was now. I also knew that I'd get kidnapped a hundred times or paint a thousand paintings if it helped my family in anyway. We could have no greater loss than the one we just experienced. This time, that gypsy's voice didn't haunt my soul anymore, it made me furious. Instead of her words scaring me as they once did, they now just made me so mad. I cursed at her as loud as I could, as if she was actually right there to hear every hateful word that was sent in her direction.

I was in such rage at that old woman as if she killed Sammy herself. We all barely got through his funeral but somehow we did. As the men from the gravesite started shoveling dirt on my brother's coffin, it started to drizzle once again. Jacob and I dared not move, just like when we wouldn't leave the river fishing. Drizzle, rain or monsoon, we didn't care. We were going to be with our buddy until the absolute very end. I don't know if it was Sammy or God himself crying after seeing us there that day. I don't know if it was Sammy's way of signaling to his family that he was okay, but either way, once again it started raining harder. I looked up at the fast-moving scars in the sky this time and fully realized without any doubt that this was the worst day of my life. This was the greatest of all great losses.

Sir, Yes Sir

After Sammy's death and all of the aftermath that most definitely comes after someone you love dies, I tried to go back to school. For lack of being able to describe it any better way, I simply didn't care about painting or art or even school anymore, so I dropped out and went back home. I even tried to go to our local university, Virginia Commonwealth University, for a while but that didn't work either. Almost everything I learned about art or really life itself, I did so to be able to teach it to Sammy and now he wasn't here anymore. I truly didn't see any possible use or enjoyment in what I once did.

I often thought that if in some twisted sort of way, the only reason that I ever learned how to paint or learn anything at all about art was to eventually help my family pay for my brother's funeral then that was more than worth it. For me, it was time to let it go because it hurt too much to keep holding on. I knew I couldn't just sit around and do nothing, and now that I had basically failed out of college twice, the only thing I felt there was left for me to do was join the military. They say traumatic experiences or even death itself causes the survivors to become closer. It's not that we didn't try, it's just that neither my parents, Jacob nor myself were ever the same again afterwards and that saying didn't seem to apply to us.

We just had too big of a hole in our own respective hearts for it to be any different. Each of us seemed to walk around going through the motions in that numbness that death so often brings. We still loved each other very much and we knew we needed each other more than ever but none of us, to include my parents, knew what to do to change it. The goal of each day seemed more about just getting through it than anything else. After a few months of this, the feelings I had about school began to apply to my home as well. It was probably out of selfishness, but the more I was there, the more I thought about Sammy and I was just too immature to handle it.

I did the only thing that I thought would take me away as far as I could get and that was to join the military. My beautiful parents fully understood that I had to get away to find myself again. They probably wished they could do the same as well, but as they sent me off, I knew that I was going in with much more than a chip on my shoulder. When there's talk about someone having a chip on their shoulder, there's usually an assumption that they have something to prove. If that's the case, I had something quite the opposite on my shoulders.

I was smart enough not to disobey orders or any other directions from the many military superiors, but the simple fact is, I didn't care there either. I didn't care about whatever they ordered me to do, and in truth, I didn't care about my own life. When I packed up to leave, I must have packed that numbness with me instead of a chip. I had Sammy's death and my family's pain on my shoulders, and for myself and those around me, that was some pretty hazardous baggage. The lack of regard for anything or really anyone actually helped me thrive a great deal in the military.

It was also the driving force in me volunteering for any and everything that was ever presented. There's an old saying that everyone who has ever enlisted knows and that is, "Never volunteer for anything." I truly didn't give a damn because I didn't care if I lived or died. I was just still trying to get through each day the best I could. The more I did and the more dangerous it was, the happier I was because those days didn't seem to possess the same amount of agony in them and definitely went by much quicker than the rest of them did.

Any Volunteers?

I fully realize that everyone has a story and everyone's story is just as valid to their lives as mine is. In saying that, I must acknowledge that the military did give me enough compassion once again to realize this fact. But before that realization happened, a habit of carelessly volunteering for everything that came along got me deployed to the Middle East for two long years, smack dab at the forefront of a war. The more dangerous the mission was, the quicker I'd raise my hand to go. I received so many accolades and medals because of my haphazardness but none of that mattered to me. That's not what I was doing it for. All of what I did was just increasingly dangerous ways to hide from the feelings that consumed me about Sammy's death every single day of my life.

I recklessly took hostages without back up, I jumped out of helicopters when I didn't need to, I even acted like I couldn't find my chemical warfare gear while running to the front of the action. All of those stupid things that I got so many medals for just didn't matter. I didn't want a medal, I wanted that damn pain off of my shoulders one way or the other. To make matters worse, we lost a lot of people over there as well. Some were as unexpected as Sammy and some were even from suicide; those were often from the people who were fighting their own losing battles with their own individual demons taking control and leading the way.

So many people who were much better and deserving of life than I was perished while, for some reason, I was left alive to do more and more careless and downright stupid things with my life. In reality, it was my own attempt to end it in my own way. The one man I did let in was Master Sergeant Huff, a wonderful man who we called Sarge. He was the father over there that all of us needed so badly. I knew that I wasn't the only one fighting to forget a life story but Sarge's story got him killed. His death was almost as bad on me as Sammy's but we had to keep going. We always had to keep going.

Death occurred on such a regular basis that it almost became a weekly if not daily part of my life and what once seemed only on my shoulders, permeated through everything I was. The more things hurt, the more numb I became and the more ridiculously dangerous things I volunteered for. All of that death changes a person and it all began with *The Armageddon* and most of all, with the "Great Loss." Death had become just as much a part of me as anything else ever was. I wrote my parents and I even wrote Jacob and they wrote me back. I definitely missed them even though I knew now more than ever I didn't want anyone that I ever loved to see me this way.

The one thing that I did feel I had right was I never dismissed another life as just an enemy. I hurt for them almost as much as I did for the ones I knew, but war evidentially happens and evidentially, lives have to end as well. It's like playing a deadly game that you really don't realize is deadly at all until someone isn't there anymore. Now death had become the unfortunate and unexpected perennial theme of my life, as that old gypsy woman said it would. Life itself seemed to be less valuable than ever before. I loaded body bag after body bag of my friends onto C-5 Galaxies, which provided their final ride home in a much different way than ever expected.

When I had to do that terrible job, I'd always look up at the sky and the clouds. Now more than ever I only saw scars, deep infuriating scars from Sammy but also from all of those young people who also died way too early. I didn't think I'd ever get back to normal and I also never forgot that old gypsy woman's words when she told me that I'd be in a great war. I often thought to myself, *Why did her evil words always have to be right?* When she told me that I'd be in a war, that was the one thing that helped me have doubt because I didn't think there was any way in hell that I'd ever join the military, but once again, she was tragically proven right.

When we did get out of that hellish place I couldn't go directly home. I was based in Spain prior to the war and had to stay there for a while longer instead of using my leave to go home because I still didn't feel worthy of being around my family after what had been happening over the past two years. I had to clear my mind first, but more importantly, I had to find a way to cleanse my soul to some degree as well. I often asked God why it had to be Sammy, and later with so many of my friends, I repeated that exact same question. I often wished in each case it would have been me instead of them, especially Sammy, but it wasn't, so somehow and in some way I had to do what Sammy made sure the fish did after we caught them. I had to figure out a way to "live on."

Life never made a great deal of sense to me before and now it definitely didn't, but after traveling throughout Europe for a while, I felt I was as ready as I ever would be to go back home, back to my real home once again. Before making my final decision to actually get there, my father had made up my mind up for me and he did so in a letter. Ready or not, I was going home and I was finally going to see those that I loved the most, at least the ones who were left anyway.

Grocery Shopping

After the war, it had been almost three years since I'd actually been home. I talked to my family on the phone when I could and I also wrote them, but to a degree, I was still procrastinating about going to see them. Death had taken so much from me and to say I was confused was as much of an understatement as any that has ever been spoken. What totally stopped my delay in its tracks and finalized my timing was a very unexpected letter from my father. I could tell in the way it was written that his words were only meant for my eyes but he not only wanted me to see them, he also wanted me to follow his directions.

Other than with his immediate family, my father was somewhat of a private man. He stayed out of other people's business and expected them to stay out of his as well. He was a smaller man in stature unlike his boys were later in life, but he was tough. His forearms seemed every bit as big and muscular as Popeye's were but his weren't cartoonish at all. They probably came from years and years of carrying around all different types of animal carcasses at his job as a meat cutter, carcasses that were most likely kept in a meat locker very similar to the one I was locked in after being kidnapped in Israel. Regardless of his petite yet powerful appearance, he was quite humble and soft-spoken but by no means timid or shy in any way.

My father detested when Jacob and I fought when we were younger. My mother knew it and thank goodness she hid most of what actually happened between us from him. There were times like when Jacob and I tried to kill each other in the back yard in front of our old nosey neighbors that he did get involved, but his interactions in regards to our fights were rare. Most of his fatherly guidance at our family dinners were directed more towards forgiveness and patience. He had a way about him that made people listen, not just his family, but anyone who he ever spoke to as well. He didn't speak many words, but when he did, he made them all count.

I knew he was proud that I joined the military but I also knew through his letter that he was worried that it changed me, too. He always seemed to know more than he let on and only let us know what he actually knew when he needed to. He was raised by a very stern father himself on a farm in a small, rural town in North Carolina. I'm sure that's where he learned his work ethic from. He always told his children that he felt oppressed to a degree growing up and he didn't want that for us.

He wanted us to follow the rules, especially his and my mother's, but he also wanted us to go out into the world and not only make our own marks but to also actually experience what he felt his hard work gave us the right to discover. His feelings towards raising his children in a different manner was really a great way of parenting. We got in trouble at home with each other, but really, most of that was hidden by our mother and we didn't do anything bad in public out of respect for both of our parents. We were more afraid of disappointing them than we ever were about any actual punishment. I think that's why it hurt Jacob and I so badly that day they locked us out of the house. It hurt bad enough to keep us from fighting for quite a while after that, and that was a lot for us.

Regardless of patience, humility or his disdain for fighting, every man comes to a time where he has to draw his own line in the proverbial sand. My father's line was protectively drawn at the back exit of a grocery store down the street from our house. My father hardly ever did the grocery shopping for the family, but on this particular day, my mother was out of town on a rare business trip and thank God she was. To my knowledge, my mother was only away from us that long twice—that week and the week that she took Sammy to Disney World.

While he was pushing the cart around in the store, he was doing the best he could to keep his very rambunctious children corralled around him or at least on the same aisle. I'm guessing Jacob was around four-years-old and he must have gotten tired of shopping because he decided to break away from the group and go out on his own adventure. It didn't take my father any more than a minute to realize that his youngest son wasn't where he was supposed to be. The second he became fully aware that Jacob had ran off, all of us started yelling out for him, "Jacob, Jacob! Where are you?"

Jacob was just right there with us, but he wasn't anymore. The more we called out, the more silent the store seemed to become. As my father thoroughly checked each aisle, he was visually becoming more worried. As his face was turning a deeper shade of red, we all heard a muffled cry from the back of the store, "Help me daddy, help me." My father used all of the power in his forearms and everywhere else in his body and soul to scoop Sammy and I up in his arms like we weighed nothing and sprinted to the back of the store where he heard Jacob's cries for help come from.

As he reached his destination, we saw a huge stringy-haired man covered in tattoos carrying Jacob out of the store's back exit door with his hand over Jacob's little mouth. This man must have been about three hundred pounds and at least six foot four, but it simply didn't matter to my father. I can't say that I ever knew what that man's true intentions were, but my father didn't ask. When my father reached that giant man, there was barely anything left of him. One punch after another struck that big man's face, body and also all of his possible intentions. My father didn't stop until the man was barely breathing, and this time, the police came for him.

It was like David and Goliath in theory, but in fact, it was more like David all the way. I didn't really understand what could have happened until later on in life, but when I was old enough to understand, my heart dropped on one hand and my pride and respect in my father rose to the heights of the sky on the other. I just knew my father was going to get arrested that day, but again, not being privy to his conversation with the policeman once again, that's not what happened. The police arrested that tattooed man instead.

Golden Child

Parent's often say they don't have a favorite child, and that may or may not be true, but at a minimum, if they have multiple children, one of them is usually a little more like one of the parents than the other. For my mother and father, Sammy was understandably the one that they spent the most time with but Jacob was much more like my father than I was, especially after what happened at the grocery store that day. Jacob was so close to our father that I jokingly referred to him as the golden child. He and my father were a little more industrious and usually a lot more even-tempered. There were exceptions, like the man at the grocery store for my father and like with me for Jacob, but for the most part, that's the way they were, just like each other.

In describing my mother and myself, I would have to say our persisting traits included being a little more vocal, excitable and even confrontational at times. Where Jacob and my father hid their emotions most of the time, me and my mother often displayed them, and many times, those displays were unfortunately in public when we thought that we or someone else had been wronged in some way. A perfect example of my mother's reactionary nature was one evening on her way from work.

She saw a man in a tie and a really nice car almost carelessly cause an accident from being on his phone while speeding through traffic about three streets from our house. Being equipped with all of her good vs. evil theology, she honked her horn at the careless driver. This must have angered the brave man because he gave my mother the finger, the same one that Jacob so often pointed at me when he was younger and then proceeded to follow her home, all while driving very close to her bumper the whole way there. For some reason, my father was already home and all of us were sitting on the front porch waiting for her. As she parked, this very unknowing man got out of is shiny, silver Mercedes and began yelling at her.

Now, we already knew what our father could do if he chose to, but by this time, all of her boys were in high school. We were also pretty tough ourselves, somewhat built and very protective over our mother. Both Jacob and I tried to jump up after we heard all of the ruckus that this idiot was directing at our mother. Before either of us got chance to actually help in anyway, my father stopped us before we ever got off of the steps. We just figured he wanted to take care of business himself, but he didn't. He just laughed and told us to sit back down and watch. This incident never got physical but I know for a fact that loud, rude man that followed our mother home wished he never did.

That fancy-dressed man got back into his fancy little car like a scolded hound and got out of our neighborhood as fast as he could after my mother finished setting him straight. My mother almost never cussed and she definitely didn't want her children to either, but that day, I think she used every word she had ever learned as an exclamation and response to that rude man following her home. He had to realize that he took the wrong road home in following our very excitable mother home that day. Both of my parents seemed like they could get crazy if they had to, and as she walked past all of us who were still sitting in shock on the porch, she winked at my dad and he giggled at her.

I already knew she was a butt whipping kind of mother, so I knew that man was lucky that words were all he got that day. I also knew she had much more back-up on the porch than that man probably ever knew. Jacob and I might have messed with each other but we knew better than to ever mess with our parents. The thoughts about going home made me remember all of the many stories that my very unorthodox, but loving family had. The letter that my father sent me was basically telling me in his way that it was time for me to get my butt home before he sicced my mother on me.

It didn't matter to him that I was a Sergeant in the military now. It didn't matter that I just got back from a war and was trying to work through a few issues. All that mattered to him was I was his son, a son that had been away from his family for way too long. Because of his insistence, at first I thought that something was wrong with either him or my mother, but as I read on, I was assured that wasn't the issue. They were doing as well as they could, they just wanted to see me as soon as possible. I had thirty days of leave left and being that this urgent request was from my father, I didn't see how I could put off going home any longer. I still had some demons floating around in my head from the war and really still from Sammy as well, but this was a very reasonable invitation that I just couldn't refuse.

Japan or Home

On the plane ride home, I had to wear my uniform in order to get a free flight on a commercial plane. The military flights had too many stops in between for me to get home in a timely manner, so I chose to fly commercial. As some of the passengers saw all of those medals that I never felt I deserved, many mistakenly identified me as a hero. From their gratitude and good intentions, mixed drink after mixed drink literally came pouring in as their appreciative gestures to me. I drank so many of those damn toxic drinks that I missed my connecting flight once I reached the States. I ended up wasting a day of my leave because of my ignorance and losing another day away from my family as well.

When I finally arrived the next day, even though it was a day later than planned, my greatly missed family was there to warmly welcome me with open arms. My mother almost pushed people out of the way to make it to me first. I thought she was going to tackle me, but instead, she gave me the longest and tightest hug that I ever had. My father was next and his tight squeeze wasn't very far behind on the pressure meter either. When it was Jacob's turn, he and I more or less patted each other on the back with one trying to be cooler that the other but we were still very glad to see each other as well.

When I arrived back at my parents' house, it didn't seem like home anymore, at least not at first. My mother understandably re-arranged everything in every room of the house—no doubt to probably make things easier on her after Sammy passed—but also because it had been three years since I'd been there, so things were bound to change a bit. I had so many wonderful memories from my childhood and I was really glad to be home, it just took my mind a little longer to get there than it did for my body to arrive. I knew that I came home with some pretty terrible baggage but I also knew that I left with some, too. I felt in time, though, that I had to fight any negative emotion that I may have felt for my family and also for myself.

After the first two weeks, that much sought-after relief actually started to come, and I have to say, I thoroughly enjoyed being home and being with my family once again. I guess it took a little time to brush off all of that death and confusion that I was experiencing before I got there. It looks like I'd been running away from the solution all along, because if things needed brushing off, my mother and father always had a broom that was most definitely constructed with a love big enough for any necessary cleaning that me or my brothers may have ever needed.

Before I left Spain, my boss let me in on some inside information about where I would be based next, and for me, going to Japan was at the forefront of my mind. I knew my orders would be coming in soon but I didn't want anyone to know about where the military would be sending me next because truthfully, I didn't want to think about being away from them for that long once again. Just when I started to get used to being home, it seemed like it was time to leave again. Before I left, towards the end of my time there, some of my old high school friends wanted to take me to the beach for the weekend.

At first, I didn't want to go, but I hadn't spent any time with them in so many years either that I caved in and went. While I was at the beach, and to definitely complicate matters, I met the most beautiful and charming woman that I had personally ever met in my life. This girl had me smitten from the first second that our eyes made contact. I may have just been naïve but I honestly think those feelings went in both directions. Her name was Emily and I couldn't help myself. Now I had met this girl, settled into being back home, was thoroughly enjoying my family and friends, and wouldn't you know it, it was time to leave again.

This time, I'd not only be going on a six-hour flight back to Spain, but in a very short amount of time, I would be going even farther on a thirteen-hour flight to Japan and staying there for four years. Neither this new girl nor my family had a clue about my next assignment or how far away it was. They didn't know how long I would be there either and all of those thoughts scattered recklessly through my head and bothered me a great deal, although it appeared there wouldn't be anything that I could do about it. I'd probably never see Emily again and God only knows what changes would take place with my family while I was gone this time. I wished I was brave enough just to get out of the military but I simply wasn't. I didn't really know how to do anything else and I still wasn't interested in anything that had to do with art. I'd come a long way but not quite that far.

I hadn't finished college and I was falsely too proud to take any old job or live in my parents' attic once again. There was a true part of me that wanted to come back home for good but then there was an equal side that accepted my all but certain future that would lead me to Japan. Because I had to re-enlist to accept my orders, I wanted to wait as long as I could before signing if for no other than to pretend like I had a real choice. My last month in Spain flew by no matter how hard I fought it, and either way, a final decision had to be made.

Jacob's The Hero

While I was at home I did get a chance to spend a little time with Jacob. Everything seemed fine, as fine as we've ever been anyway. We were never overly close, and unfortunately, it still seemed to be that way. He would be graduating himself soon, and in doing so, once again beating me at something else. He was going to school full-time and he was in a very challenging engineering program while still working full-time as well. He had also met a nice girl who I'm fairly sure he was planning on making a life with sometime in the not too far off future. Regardless of any of our feelings towards each other, I've clearly known and often said that he was as close to Sammy as I was, it was just in his own way.

It may not have been through spending time with him, fishing or working on art projects but he absolutely spent as much time with Sammy as anyone else did, to include me. Their time together was usually spent on more technical types of activities. Jacob could work on and fix just about anything and often made whatever he fixed better than it was when it was brand new. He fixed cars, lawnmowers, computers and really anything that he wanted to.

He was getting a civil engineering degree from VCU to someday soon design and build roadways and bridges. That was the second college that I failed out of, but instead of feeling jealous, I was really proud of him. VCU was fifteen minutes away from my parents' house and even though I'm sure he could have went to college anywhere he wanted to, he chose to stay at home and help our parents out through all those years of sadness after Sammy died. I didn't do that. I ran away and didn't feel like I helped them at all. That fact is probably going to be something that will always haunt me, but something that I'll always have to live with too.

With anything that Jacob did, he took whatever time was needed to make what he was working on as perfect as he could. I know Jacob's future will be full of success and contentment because he really deserves it. Even though I was the oldest brother, if I was truthful with myself, I knew regardless of the lifetime of contempt that he had for me, he always acted much wiser and even more mature than I ever did. He was the one smart enough to call the rescue squad when Sammy got hurt on the river that day. His intelligence and quick thinking had them waiting for us at the dock when *The Armageddon* pulled up with our hurt, but precious middle brother onboard. He was also the one who stayed with our family for those many years while I didn't.

I honestly, from the bottom of my heart, felt that Jacob was the real and true hero of our family. I knew the past was the past and I remember it well, but the unquestionable feelings that I now have for my youngest brother are only that of appreciation and love. We may never have a conversation where my feelings are every fully disclosed, but it doesn't matter because it's the truth. My mother may not have liked us cussing or fighting but the one thing that she never put up with on any level was lying to her or anyone else. She said all that lies do is create other lies which were needed to keep up with the original lies, and it was just too much. She wanted her boys to be truthful with others and to themselves at all times no matter what.

Following my mother's directions about lies, I felt I had to be as absolutely truthful with myself, and when I was, I came to the full realization that Jacob was really a great person. While at home, I saw that he basically adopted Puddles as his own and I couldn't think of a better second choice to be that dog's new owner if it couldn't be Sammy. Jacob and I were total opposites in many ways, to include what we did with Sammy, but if you think about it, we were very much separate but equal in many ways as well.

A story that still cracks me up to this day and one that highlights Jacob's prevailing maturity over me was one of those days, lying in the field down the street searching for sky boobies like we often did back then. Sammy, as he very frequently did when we went anywhere, had to use the bathroom almost as soon as we got there. This time, being that we were outside in a field near a patch of woods, and thankfully being that he just had to go number one, I told him to just go to the edge of the woods and pee. Sammy didn't have a problem doing something he'd done at least a thousand times in the woods before, so he went over to the first tree he could find.

Regardless of what number he went, whether it was number one or two, he always had to pull his pants all the way down to his ankles before he did his business. Before he got a chance to get them all the way down, he let out this bloodcurdling scream. It was so loud that the birds that were perched in the nearby trees immediately took flight, and it seemed like Jacob and I did, too, trying to get to him as fast as we could. At first, I thought he may have gotten bitten by a snake or something like that, but when we got over to him, it wasn't quite the kind of snake we were thinking about. In fear and in his obvious and visual confidence, Sammy had his private parts in his hand trying to shake something off of the end of it.

I didn't know what in the hell to say about that or what to do about it either. Jacob, in his much calmer and more mature demeanor did, however. Jacob bent down to see what Sammy was so upset about, but before he got all the way to the problem, Sammy yelled out, "There's an eye on it!" I still didn't know exactly what was wrong with his manhood but I knew that it was still in his hand and he wasn't very happy with whatever was on it that he thought was an eye. Once I realized that it couldn't be but so serious of an issue, and since I was fairly sure that he didn't grow another eye in the wrong place, I couldn't do anything other than laugh and I laughed a lot.

It was one of those laughs that almost made me cry and I just couldn't stop or help myself at all. Sammy saw absolutely no humor in his newly-discovered problem, and after a solution was found, he didn't talk to me much the rest of the day either. It took Jacob to finally settle him down and discover that what Sammy thought was an extra eye was actually a tick that found a temporary home in a place that Sammy very much wanted it evicted from immediately. I tried to help him, I really did, but I was laughing so hard I wasn't any real help at all. While Jacob did the best he could in holding back his own laughter, he exterminated that terrible eye that upset Sammy so much.

That was a less serious and very comical remembrance about how Jacob always saved the day, but funny or not, he truly was always our family's hero. After that brotherly adventure, we returned our eyes back to the clouds and our backs to the field where we started. For the rest of that day, all Sammy told us that he saw in the clouds were stupid ticks and floating mean eyes. Thinking about how my mother would have handled the situation, I remembered she used to burn ticks off of us when we discovered them. Given the sensitive nature of Sammy's issue, I'm sure glad we didn't bring her method up to him that day.

Israel Rain

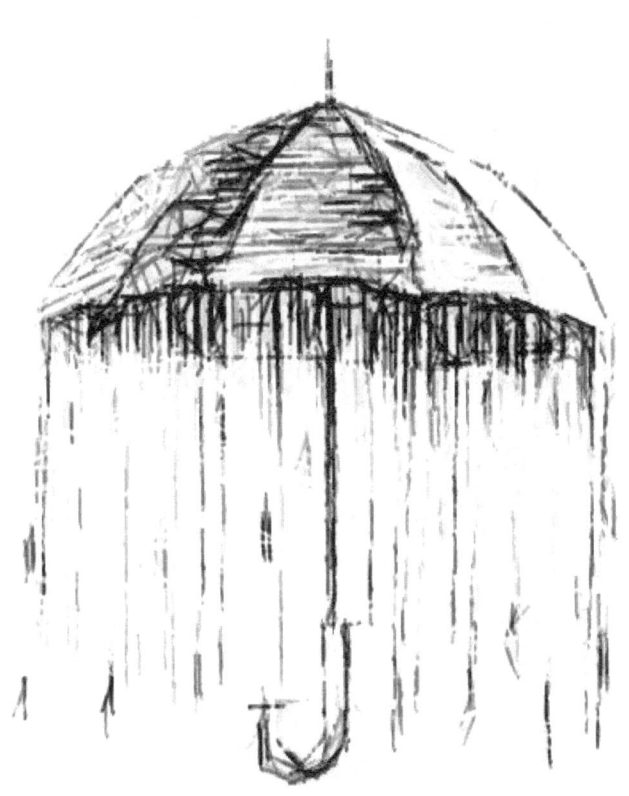

With the decision about my future being at its final hour, I thought a lot about Jacob, Sammy, my parents and even my own name. My parents told me the reason I was named Israel was, before they had children—which probably meant when they still had a little money—they actually visited that very complex country. They wanted their wonderful experience in that holy place to always be a part of their lives, so their first child's name was settled long before they ever thought about having kids. I'd never tell them that I got kidnapped in their favorite place or that I was accosted by a seemingly all-knowing old gypsy woman, one that mysteriously and correctly seemed to see all of the worst events of all of our lives long before they ever happened.

No matter what happened, there I was, very grateful that they gave me a very meaningful name that was so relative to my actual life. I often felt that I didn't live up to my name but I also felt that my namesake didn't either. Both me and the country still seemed to be very much a work in progress. History tells us that the country made numerous mistakes throughout many generations, some of those often led to their people being forced to run away from their homeland.

Considering its past, I simply didn't see how I was any different. There are so many comparisons between my life and the country that it's almost uncanny. To me, Sammy was our family's Wailing Wall. He, like one of the holiest places in Israel—or on the Earth for that matter—had a profoundness about him that was unmatched, just like the Wailing Wall did. Jacob reminded me of Mt. Zion because he was always the foundation of sensibility when it came to us three and often came up with the solution to so many of the things that our family faced as well. This went for past issues and would no doubt be the same way in the future as well. My parents were like Zatima's to me, that was the small café that served those wonderful desserts.

That place existed for over two hundred years and never even closed a single second of any day along the way. My parents were similar to that historical place because, just like that café that never closed, both of my parents were always there for us no matter what ever happened or when it was. Zatima's, or at least their food, was there for me during my kidnapping, and similarly, no matter if the situation was good or bad, so were my parents for their children.

They were even like those delicious desserts in that all of their efforts and all of those years of working so hard were to make sure their children always had the best that they could provide. The café only served coffee and those awesome treats but my parents always served so much more. They freely gave out unconditional love and guidance that sometimes had to be a challenge, given the way that Jacob and I often acted towards each other. There was no question that they corrected our shortcomings, especially my mother towards me when Jacob would jump out of that stupid coat closet after hitting himself in the face.

Even with those lessons, she somehow turned them into special gifts of knowledge that were delivered with the desire for her children to act in such a way that would aid them to be able to handle whatever life threw at them, no matter whether we considered them to be fair or not. All three brothers were as different as night and day, and even though they'd never admit it, they loved us differently. It wasn't a bad different, it was more like how my mother ran Christmas. None of our presents were the exact same. They were chosen based on our needs and wants at the time and very much equal in value. They probably wouldn't feel the same way but I knew I never took my parents for granted.

I may not have always listened as I should have at first but I was never unappreciative for all they did and gave up for us. Being at home for that month made me realize how blessed my life really had been, regardless of what happened in the war or really anywhere else. At one time, I thought I was like the overall country of Israel itself with its many languages and divisions. I was full of confusion and strife but I still had so many possibilities of a beautiful future, just like the country is promised if they make the correct decisions. I didn't see it that way at the time but I still knew that a full life, the one my parents wanted for me, was just out there hiding from me for a while.

I didn't care enough to look for it before then but now I do. Not so long ago I was running away in fear and rage from the scars on Sammy's body and then from his unexpected death but I was also running from the many scars that were inside of my own heart as well. That accident and Sammy not getting out of bed that day or ever again set something off inside of me, something I'd been running away from ever since. Thank God, and with much credit given to my visit home, I now feel more like that old building that I was taken to by that frumpy salt-and-pepper-haired taxi driver.

That building, like myself, started out as a mess, but as we went deeper into it, not only did the carpet and the surroundings become more amicable, so did my heart. I didn't understand it at the time but everything that I ever experienced led me to be able to make the biggest decision of my life. In a way, to expand on my feelings about the future, I also now feel like the river Jordan. I'm alive and flowing forward again and I can now once again be able to be the source of other people's nourishment as well. In thinking about Israel, there is no way not to mention Jesus. He was born for a very specific purpose and I absolutely prayed that I was as well. My purpose may not have been as important to mankind as his was but I strongly felt that it could help many others none the less.

As the final day came to make my decision about staying in the military or going home for good, I felt that wonderful country, my name, a pretty girl and the incredible family that I was so blessed to be a part of made up my mind up for me. Scared or not, I'd be a Sergeant in the military no more. I declined my orders to Japan, and as me and my brothers often did when we were younger, I looked at the clouds in the sky once again and began looking forward to the future, a future that I finally looked forward to having.

Not Again

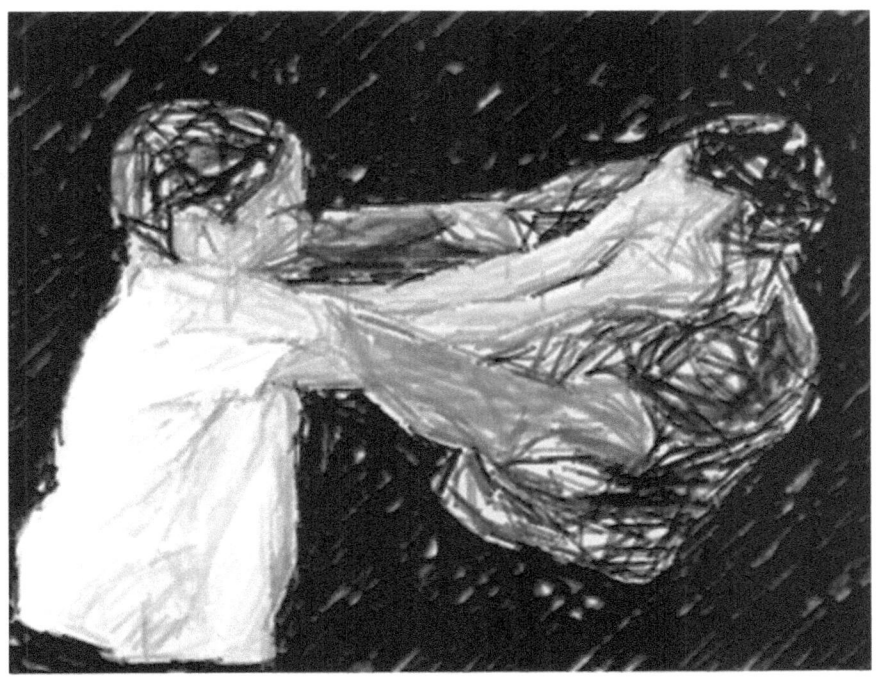

B ack at home, I humbled myself and moved back in parents' attic. I started dating my beautiful Emily and I got a job that would have to be good enough for the time being to get started with my new life. I packed a little fear with the other luggage that I brought back home, but I was handling it. I even started taking classes again in hopes of not failing out for the third time. Being home this time almost felt like it did from the days of my youth with, of course, one very special person missing. The way I handled my single exception was to finally realize that Sammy was in a much better place, doing a much more important job, with a much more knowledgeable and bigger family in heaven.

Jacob and I didn't even seem to really have any issues this time because, just like me, he was at school or work or with his own girlfriend most of the time. When we were around each other, we acted more like the adults that we very much were by then. I did have some small health issues left over from the war that I was getting taken care of at the Veteran's hospital. Just little things like shin splints that I never got treated and a slight tear in my meniscus but even those issues were beginning to heal after I actually took the time to take care of them. Things were pretty good and I knew I wanted them to stay that way.

This time, with my own newly-discovered maturity, running away from anything wasn't an option. I was home, and I was home for good, so I had to make the most out of my life. The one problem I did have was, because I sold my truck before I left for the military, I still hadn't quite made enough money to buy another one yet. I was working on it and, believe it or not, Jacob let me use his car when he didn't need it. Often times, as long as I dropped him off wherever he needed to be and I put gas in the tank, he didn't have a problem with me borrowing one of his past big Christmas gifts. It was on one of those chauffeuring trips that I had to drop Jacob off at the doctor's office before I could use his car for the rest of the day.

A regular doctor is a far cry from appointments at the Veteran's hospital. When I had an appointment there it was usually an all-day event, but since Jacob's appointment should only take about an hour at the most—and I had to pick him back up anyway—I decided to wait for him in the parking lot. I planned to listen to the radio in his car until he finished. I wanted to catch up on the music that I hadn't regularly heard in quite a while and especially didn't hear in Spain, the desert or in Israel.

I lost track of how much time had passed at first, but when I looked down at my watch, I realized that he had been inside for well over two hours instead of the expected hour. I decided to go into the doctor's office to see what was taking him so long. At first I have to admit I thought he may be playing another trick on me. I thought maybe he took an Uber home without me seeing him, leaving me, his idiot brother, in the parking lot for hours singing to the air like a bone head. I thought we were past all of that, but I wasn't sure, so I decided to investigate. When I walked in the doctor's office, I asked the nurse at the front desk if she knew when Jacob Rain would be finished.

After I asked her, I noticed that her face became flushed; that was the look that something was wrong that I've seen before. I didn't think anyone there would have scolded her like the well-dressed man did to the taxi driver in that old building in Israel, but I definitely had seen that shade of red before. She asked me what relation I was to Jacob, and after I told her I was his brother and his ride home, she checked a notebook on her desk, purposefully delaying her response until she found the most appropriate way to tell me where he was. When she felt she had what she needed to answer my question, she carefully told me that he was admitted into the hospital about thirty minutes ago.

The ambulance evidentially left out of the back of the doctor's office without me seeing it and obviously with no one telling me anything was going on with Jacob. I thought, *What the hell? I just drove him there in his own car and he seemed to be just fine.* I thought he was going to the doctor just to get a physical for his final semester of college but now he'd been admitted to the hospital. I called my parents to let them know what the nurse said and what hospital Jacob was in. I didn't know what else to say because I didn't know anything else. As I parked in the same stupid parking lot, at the same stupid hospital that I did when Sammy got hurt, my parents pulled in right after me.

We found out that not only was he already admitted, he was in his own room by then, too. When we were told that he was in room 622, we all headed to the sixth floor as fast as we could. In the elevator the look of worry that was seen way too many times in my parents' faces over the years was the prevailing sight once again. Jacob's room was right across from the elevators, so when the doors opened, we could immediately see that the doctor was in there with him. I experienced what I didn't welcome as Déjà vu as the doctor clearly explained why Jacob had to be admitted to the hospital in such an abrupt fashion.

For the first time in a long time, I thought about that old gypsy woman once again. I thought all of the terrible things that she said would happen had already happened and I was more than ready to get on with the better parts of my life that she also spoke about instead of being at the hospital with a sick or hurt brother again. I hated feeling that she must have forgotten another chapter to my already very long book of unexpected tragedies, sicknesses and wars. As the doctor told us and Jacob what he needed and how quickly he needed it, I once again cussed that old woman if nowhere else than in my mind.

Sergeant Santa

To make things worse, it was right around Christmas time when all of this was happening. The week before, my mother made it a point to let us all know that she was planning on making it her favorite time of year once again, like it used to be when her boys were young and all of us were still here. I know my coming home helped get her excitement back but now I'm sure she didn't look at Jacob being in the hospital or what he needed as something to celebrate. My mother always gave us one big gift as the finale of our Christmas day. Now more than ever, I was glad that I was like my mother and I knew I needed to do what she would do.

Since I had already been getting treatment from the Veteran's hospital, most of the doctors there knew that I wasn't active duty military anymore but that didn't stop any of my plans. After I left the hospital, I went home and back up to the attic. I riffled through my old duffle bag that I hadn't fully unpacked as of yet and pulled out my dress blues. I reached back in the deep, tightly-packed green bag and also pulled out a wooden box that contained every medal I ever received for all of those things I did in the military trying to end my own life. I gingerly pressed my uniform to perfection and took a razor out and straightened up my hair as well. Once I thought my uniform was just right, I put it on and slowly attached all four rows of medals across my chest.

I still never believed I deserved any of them but I knew someone who did. If it took me wearing them once again to help my brother, then that was what I was going to do. My parents were still at the hospital with Jacob, who had to stay there two days at a minimum, so no one saw me as I left the house and got into his car and headed towards the Veteran's hospital. On the ride there, I realized that I was on the most important mission of my life and my brother's, too. I parked right in front of the emergency room and walked inside. As I walked in, it was like when an American walked into the wrong place in the desert; there was complete silence and everyone turned to look.

I ignored my personal unworthiness as my medals were sending their intended message and my plan started to work. The nurse at the check-in desk got two doctors the second I asked to speak to one. In great appreciation for what was being so majestically presented across my chest, they all absolutely treated me as if I was a visiting king. When I told my wishes to the two doctors, they didn't hesitate in finding a way to start making it happen that night. I was tested for one thing after the other like Jacob had been hours before and the results of those tests were what I prayed for them to be.

This wasn't just for Jacob, although, if it would have been, I would have done it just as fast. This was for my father, the remembrance of Sammy, Puddles, myself and most definitely for my mother, too. She was always our Santa and so much more, but this time, I would have to be Jacob's. I guess you could even call me Sergeant Santa for the time being. My test and the doctor's comparisons went well into the night, but once everything was thoroughly evaluated, a date two days later was set. Jacob should be back home himself by then and I was hoping to be able to give him the news that I knew he had to be waiting for.

Jacob always stayed and took care of everyone else and it was time that someone took care of him. Our past didn't matter at all anymore. He was the only brother I had left and I know without a shadow of a doubt that he would have done the same for me. On the day I had to report back to the hospital, although my mother always taught me not to, I had to tell a lie. I told my family that I had an interview out of town, but if Jacob was out of the hospital, I wanted to go and I'd hurry home afterwards as fast as I could. As they always were, they were supportive of what I wanted to do and didn't have any issues with what they really didn't know they were giving their support to.

Still Pretending

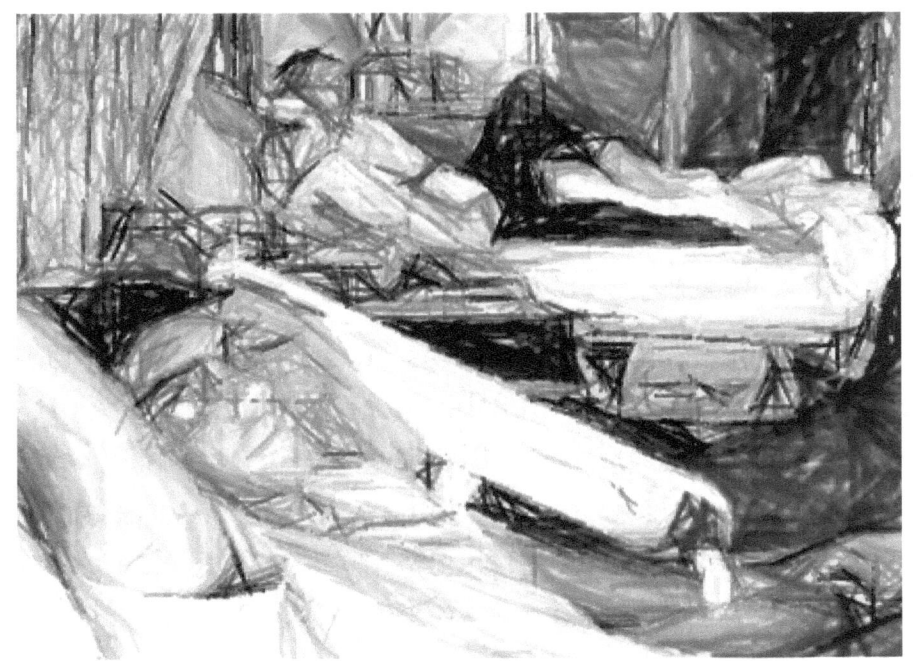

Back at my hospital, the same two doctors knew when I would be arriving and met me at the door. I didn't have to wait, and although I didn't have my uniform on this time, they still treated me as if I did. I think, instead of the medals, this time they honestly respected what I was getting ready to do for my brother. Jacob's issues most likely came from those years of him helping our parents grieve for Sammy. His blood pressure had been very high for his age for a long time, and although he didn't know that his kidneys were failing until that day he was admitted to the hospital, they had to have been silently giving him trouble for a long time.

He seemed fine, but he wasn't, and his doctor made sure that we all knew that his situation was dire. As the anesthesiologist started putting me out, a smile came across my face. Not only was I finally proud of something I was doing myself, but I felt that what I was doing was something that needed to be done to solidify Jacob's right to continue in fulfilling his mission in life as well. I was told that the surgery went on without a hitch, and although later I believed the doctors, while I was under I wasn't so sure. I didn't almost die or have any known reactions to anything but something was going on other than an operation on that operating table I was laying on.

I don't know if it was a dream or not, but as the doctors sliced into my body, I was seemingly watching them do the surgery. I didn't feel any pain or anything other than a tug on my body here and there but what I did know was I felt pride once again without question. This was a pride based on the feelings that I could finally repay the true hero of our family, at least to some small degree. I never floated through the air like some people say they do but for some strange reason, I still felt like I was completely outside of my body. At first it was as if I was watching what the doctors were doing to my motionless form but not too long after the surgery began, I seemed to drift to somewhere else.

It appeared that on the day of my surgery I also got a gift, one that was similar to what I was trying to give to Jacob. What I got, in addition to an ethereal feeling of pride, was a glimpse into what I could only begin to describe as what I thought heaven would be like. I don't know why I was given this great vision but I still to this day feel like it was because, for the first time in my life, I made a decision that was truly selfless. I was doing something that I didn't expect or even want anything back from personally. I wanted it to help Jacob but that was it. Again, I may have just been dreaming, but to me, what I saw, felt and heard was just as real as anything that I have ever experienced before.

There was such a peace and the true feelings of the great presence of the all-knowing, that it was joyously overwhelming. There was the light murmur of the most beautiful music. It was so soul-soothing that everything, wherever I was, seemed to be gently swaying in the peace and harmony that it created. I didn't necessarily see anything from the past or even what may be in the future but I did get a full look into what pure love was. Then more than ever, I was positive that Sammy, Sarge and all of those young soldiers we lost were a part of that beauty too and weren't lost anymore.

I was engulfed in an intense endearment where, even though I didn't know what the outcome of my life would be, I did know for sure that some divine, loving someone did. This was a true peace that let me fully realize that, regardless of whatever happened at the end of my story, everything would be much more than okay. That feeling was for me but it was also for me to pass on to everyone I loved as well. As I came to, about three hours after the surgeons started, I felt nothing more than what I would describe as a scratch on my side. Everything went extremely well and I knew that what was once a part of me was on the way to the other hospital to be Jacob's now.

Once my head cleared a little from being under the anesthesia, I called my parents to prove my mother right. She always said that when you told one lie, you had to tell another and that's exactly what I did. I knew I'd be leaving a message because I also knew they'd be at the hospital with Jacob when I called. I left the message saying that my interview went well and I'd be back home the next day. I was also still pretending when I said that if she wanted me to drive through the night to get home, for her to call me back and let me know. Thankfully, she didn't call back until the next morning and I was able to rest and recover throughout the night.

I knew this was pushing it but I really didn't feel I had any other option, and besides, I needed to get to Jacob's hospital as soon as I was able to, to see how he was doing. When my mother called the next morning, she told me that Jacob got the call and that his surgery went well. He, being in a regular hospital, had to stay a few more days than I did but all of his doctors were extremely confident that in a very short amount of time he'd be as healthy as a horse without dialysis and without too much rehab. When my own doctors came in to check on me, they knew what I needed to do and even though they didn't fully recommend it, they understood that I wanted to get out of there the first chance I got to get back to my family.

Every soldier, airman, marine or sailor that I ever served with had my back, as I did theirs, but these two young doctors that helped me so much did as much as anyone ever did. When they let me leave, even though it was a day or two too early than recommended, I went straight to room 622 in that other hospital to see how my little brother was doing. Life and my decision to get out of the military, along with the wonderful doctors and nurses at the Veteran's hospital set up my ability to help Jacob fix his illness almost immediately after he realized that he had one. As I walked into Jacob's hospital room, tears welled in his eyes as they did mine as well. My parents, who were with him all night, told us that they were going downstairs to the cafeteria to get something to eat.

They may have really been hungry or even thirsty but I think they were more interested in giving their sons some alone time to talk. Once we talked for a few minutes about Jacob's surgery, a kidney or any kind of health issues weren't spoken about again. My secret would be safe with me forever and now that Jacob was going to be okay, none of that seemed to matter anymore anyway. We talked like the brothers we never were before. I talked about Emily and our plans and he talked about graduating college and joked about beating me at something else.

I guess the new theme of my life was pride—the good kind too—because I was so proud that he'd get a chance to beat me at something else once again. I think I was even more relieved in knowing he'd be healthy enough to graduate but also to do so much more afterwards. We talked about how blessed we were to have the parents we had. We talked about Puddles and many of his mischievous little ways. We also talked about Sammy a lot and even that tick that had him so excited that day. By the time our parents came back into his room, we covered and forgave each other for about twenty years of everything we ever did to each other, to include The Armageddon and the BB to the butt incident.

I wondered if he had the same visons of what I thought was heaven while he was under anesthesia, even though I never asked. I hoped very much that he did because it was truly magical. My hero was lying there in that hospital bed, beginning to heal but he was also speaking and planning about the many things that he wanted to accomplish when he got out. I realized then and after I gained a certain level of maturity myself that he was very special, too. There was no telling from that point on how he'd conquer his dreams of the future but I knew without a doubt that he would.

Parents Always Know

B eing that it was Christmastime and with her two young men healing at home, one publicly and one privately, our mother returned to her own plans of making Christmas like the ones from our past come again. The closer it got to that blessed day, the more excited and enjoyable to watch she became. She knew she had a lot to be thankful for and so did my father and Jacob and I as well. Her happiness often led her into her grown children's room way too early in the morning, singing Christmas songs in efforts directed towards getting us out of bed. If her singing didn't work in getting us up, she'd then go to her back-up plan, which just happened to be named with the same name as my old Jon boat was.

If we didn't rise and shine when she thought we should or ignored the Christmas hymns she was singing, she'd put Puddles on the bed next to our face until he licked us awake. If that dog's slobber didn't wake us up then his Alpo breathe always would. I also noticed that two Christmas trees went up in the house that year and with what seemed like every other decoration that was ever sold in Richmond, Virginia. She wanted everyone to see her way of showing how grateful she was once again. This crazy woman made my father put so many lights on the outside of the house that I'm sure it could be seen from outer space as well.

Our mother's happy outburst made us happy and also helped both of us heal at a much faster pace than ever expected. Even though Jacob and I were fully grown, we felt like little boys once again and it was kind of nice. Instead of Sammy's death being so raw for her, she was finally at the point where she fully realized what a great gift, he was for the time that she was blessed enough to have him. When Christmas morning came, like she'd been practicing, she came into both Jacob and I's rooms to wake us up. This time, she came in with both of her options, option one and option two. She was singing and Puddles' tongue was also swiping across our respective faces, all at once. She didn't give us the least little chance not to get up when she wanted us to that Christmas morning.

Regardless of what age we ever were, and even if I was away, she always hung a stocking for everyone on the mantle, to include me and Sammy and even one for Puddles. My mom, as she always did, gathered her family and settled us in the living room, close to the bigger Christmas tree out of the pair in the house and across from those well-hung stockings. Also, as she always did, she equally presented all of what she called the smaller Christmas gifts first and directed us to open them individually and one at a time.

When Jacob and I unwrapped certain things we'd, in a respectful but sarcastic way, make fun of them by saying, "Oops undies, or sockies" and even, "Next up" as Sammy used to, but when we got our big gifts that year, the ones that in reality we were both too old to be getting, my gift seemed to be substantially more expensive than Jacob's was for the first time that I could ever remember. After my mom did her ritual preparatory cleaning, she said the ever familiar, "Boys, I think I forgot something." It was even funnier and more obvious than I remembered, but she said it anyway.

She wanted Jacob to open his big gift first, and when he did, he got four new tires for his car. Now, at our age, that was a great present because, after lending me his car so often, I knew he probably needed them and since she gave them to him for Christmas, he wouldn't have to buy them for himself. He wasn't an engineer yet and he didn't have much more money than I did, so it was a very fitting present. When it was my grown self's turn for my big gift, I was fairly sure that it wouldn't be another Jon boat but that was okay because I didn't want another one either. When she got to me, my ridiculously giddy mother told me my present was hidden in the bathroom, just like Sammy's Disney World tickets were years ago.

My whole family, to include myself, laughed remembering Sammy's last trip to the bathroom looking for his present. Just like she did for Sammy, she hid mine in the damn tank of the toilet and also in a big plastic envelope. I shook my head in amusement as I took my big gift out of the toilet tank and returned to my family in the living room. My father was more or less a spectator in the past on Christmas day because he never wanted to disturb the rhythm of the day that my mother developed so well over the years, but not this Christmas. As I was opening my envelope, he got off the couch where he was previously watching the day's events from and came over to me and put his hand on my shoulder.

I didn't know what was in that envelope at the time but I felt like I was being knighted as I looked inside of it. When the envelope was totally open there were so many one-hundred-dollar bills inside that it all added up to ten thousand dollars. I don't know who told them that I paid for Sammy's funeral but it was obvious that someone did. This time, my father gleamed with pride waiting for the perfect time to repay what he let me know was the greatest and best-timed gift that he ever received from anyone ever before or ever since. Even though the circumstances for the need were extremely sad, he knew that not only were his own prayers answered that day but he felt that he succeeded in helping me finally become a man.

I didn't know what to say because I didn't have any idea that anyone other than me and the men at the funeral home knew. I was just grateful that I had it at a time where my family was in such need and my father incorrectly questioning his worth as a father. I never expected or even wanted the money back but my hardworking father wanted to keep that debt as his own responsibility and to be his final gift to his very special middle son. My father never showed a great amount of emotion but that day his heart was so full that it caused even his eyes to become full with joyful tears as well.

My mother resisted as long as she could until she had to take the rhythm of the day back over and even she yelled out, "Next up!" herself. I thought we had finished for the day but she let me know there was one more big gift and it was also for me. As she handed me a package that was wrapped and even felt very much like how socks would be, I asked her if she really wanted to remember the last gift of the year as being sockies. She laughed and basically lovingly told me to shut up and open my last big gift. When I did, I have to admit I was a little confused because the last gift of that year was an Ace bandage. She'd wrapped toilet paper and other funny gifts in the past but I wasn't totally sure what she was trying to get at by giving me an Ace bandage or by calling it a big gift.

I tried to play along, not giving in to the fact that the Ace bandage she gave me was very much like the one I was wearing under my shirt, the same one that was helping to protect my stitches from my own secret surgery. Just like the money, this was something that they weren't supposed to know about. Jacob was looking at her as if she finally really did fall off her rocker. My mother called both of us over to her and began squeezing both of us with one of her massive hugs. She put the squeeze on us so much that I was extremely glad that Jacob spoke up and said she was hurting his side. I was relieved because she was hurting mine too.

When my mother finally let us go, she reached over to my shirt tail and raised it revealing the bandages I already had wrapped around me. As Jacob saw my bandages that were exactly the same as his, he squinted as to say, "damn, we're both falling to pieces," but he still didn't quite put two and two together. As our mother stepped back to gratefully allow a little outside air between us, she had the same tears in her eyes as my father did just moments before. She spoke out and told me, "I know." It's not that I was trying to be overly slow or was even in the dark about the matter, it's just that I didn't know exactly what or how much my parents actually knew and I didn't want to offer up any confirmations just then.

As she told both Jacob and me what she actually knew, which was pretty much everything except for the exact details at the Veteran's hospital, Jacob followed suit with the tears which, dammit, once again made me do the same. Our whole family was sitting in the living room like a bunch of babies crying from joy. That particular Christmas day brought so much to all of us. I thought in both instances I did everything I could do to help the ones that I loved the most. I tried my best to do it in private but it seemed that everyone knew everything now. She never told me who filled them in on all of my secrets but she did tell me and Jacob to sit down at the kitchen table and have a talk.

A Scar in the Sky

N ow, Jacob and I had plenty of lectures, dinners and even arguments at that kitchen table, but I can't ever say at any time in our lives did we ever just sit down and have a normal conversation about anything there. I knew what we were going to talk about couldn't actually be considered normal but I didn't want to make a big deal about either. We'd all cried enough for the day, regardless if the tears were from joy and appreciation or not. The main thing that I wanted Jacob to know was that, to me, even if he was my younger brother, I just wanted him to know that he really was my hero, and as far as I was concerned, our family's hero as well. I let him know how much I respected him for always putting our family first. Those were the times where I was the most disappointed in myself because I couldn't or didn't for whatever selfish reason.

To me, regardless of anything I may have done, he was a much greater man than I ever was, and as Sammy would say, I had to do everything in my power so he would "live on." Everything happened so fast, as it always seems to, and being that it did, even I didn't time to do anything else other than the right thing. I wanted us to be the brothers that we wouldn't allow ourselves to be when we were younger and he most definitely felt and explained his desires for the same.

He now knew what he was given but I don't think until I told him that he ever realized how much he actually gave—what he himself gave to me and to everyone else as well. I would have given him my other kidney and with it, my whole life as well if he would have needed it and I now know that he would do the same for me. We talked so long that my mother started setting the table for Christmas dinner around us. As our parents joined us at the table, we spoke less and our parents took over where we left off. Even my father was almost chatty, which absolutely never happened before then, but I think even he never knew how successful his life was before that day either.

Like I said before, we never cared about money or gifts. We always had all that we needed or even wanted right there sitting at our family's kitchen table. Since we knew our single exception this year was in a much greater place doing much greater things, even those thoughts were at peace now. Before we finished eating, my mother reminded us that, sometimes more often than not, love leaves scars. Sometimes those scars are in the sky or in our memories, sometimes they're in paintings or in our work or families and sometimes they're even on your side where your kidney used to be, but either way, as long as love "lives on," contentment and happiness in life will always eventually follow.

I knew with all of these profound lessons that our parents always wholeheartedly filled us with, that someday Jacob and I would be able to pass them on to our own children. Maybe for me, even on to that fluffy-haired, brown-eyed daughter that the old gypsy lady from Israel said I'd have some day. With all of that said and considered, if I honestly looked back at my life or even forward to my future to come, regardless of what age I am or what I may be doing, isn't that alone as good of a purpose for life as any could be?

My mother correctly said that there will always be scars in the sky and also in other places to some degree as well, but as proven throughout my story and the stories of so many others, there will never be a scar so deep or rigid that, with time, selflessness and love can't be altered to something much different than it was originally seen as. Those same scars could possibly be restored to a place where they never would have been without that original wound mysteriously guiding the temporarily unforeseen way.

*May God
Bless You*

www.ingramcontent.com/pod-product-compliance
Lightning Source LLC
Chambersburg PA
CBHW031352170626
46807CB00002B/930